MIMI ROSE

The fate of cursed roses and stolen snowflakes

book 1

To the girls who live their lives in books and fairy tales, waiting for a handsome morally Grey character to kidnap them into adventure.

To my sisters, the love I have for you is unmatched. Thank you. Those with blood and without, thank you for the support, love, and protection. I would kill for you.

Contents

Preface

Once upon a time, there was a mad king and an angelic queen who ruled over a magical world, who said every day, "Oh, if only we had an heir!" but they never received one.

Then it happened one day while the Queen was sitting under her two rose trees, one of which bore snow-white and the other red roses, that a mermaid crept out of the water onto the ground and said to her, "Your wish shall be fulfilled, and before a year passes, you will bring two daughters of the greatest power into the world,"

What the Mermaid said did happen, and the Queen gave birth to two girls who were so beautiful that the king could not contain himself for joy, and he ordered a great celebration.

He invited not only the Fae, Vampire, and Wolves, but also the Witches so that they would be kindly disposed towards the children.

The feast was celebrated with great splendour, and at its conclusion, those of power presented the child with their magic gifts. The one gave virtue, the second unnatural beauty, the third overflowing wealth, and so on, with everything that one could wish for on earth.

Another had just pronounced her blessing when the unknown demonic witch suddenly walked in. She wanted to avenge herself; she cried out with a loud voice, "In the princess's life, one shall prick herself with a thorn made from anger and fall over dead."

Even she was horrified, and so the witch frowned, looking upon the girls, Because she was unable to undo the wicked wish, but only to soften it, she said, "It shall not be her death. One princess will only fall into a sleep awakened by only the truest love."

The king, wanting to rescue his dear daughters, issued an order that all thorns in the entire kingdom should be burned. The magical gifts were all fulfilled by the girls, for both were so unnaturally beautiful, charming, and intelligent that everyone who saw them had to love them.

They were as good and happy, as busy and cheerful as ever two children in the world were, only Aria was more quiet and gentle than Melody. Melody liked better to run about in the meadows and fields seeking flowers and catching butterflies, but Aria sat at home with her mother and helped her with her housework, or read to her when there was nothing to do.

But then tragedy struck as their mother fell ill and the Mad King went even madder. Haunted by the curse, and to keep his daughters safe from the curse, the King built a tall tower deep in the gardens. He built stairs that led up to a room at the very top, a room with one window.

I

Part One

Tragic Tales Of The Tower

One

Playlist

Two

Melody

The words of tales ran through my mind, transporting me into a world far from here. The letters turned my dull life into an adventure, where I was a warrior, a lover, and a girl with unlimited choices.

Our tower was large and luxurious; it might've been a prison, but we were still princesses. My bed was filled with purple and black blankets with embroidery and too many red cushions; then I knew what to do with them. On each corner, there was a wooden pole. Although my sister had a running row of snow around hers, which she created as a child, floating mindlessly, mine had animated thorns, harmful to all but me. Each was more beautiful than the last.

'Melody,'

I groaned, trying to ignore my sister, as I held onto the feeling.

'Melody!' Her voice grew higher.

'What?' I snapped, shutting my leather-bound book.

'Look,' she said, tilting her head towards the window.

Although we were twins, our similarities stopped at our skin and bone structure. My sister's hair shimmered gold and snow white, like frost kissed by sunlight, while mine was black, streaked with deep, rose red. Her blue eyes were as clear as winter skies, a mirror of our angelic mother. On the other hand, I had the same deep purple eyes as our mad father—two disjointed halves of a single whole.

I put my book of tales on the wooden bedside table, filled with engraved flowers and images of nature. I looked at my sister; her grin was too great for this early, and her pink smile made my lips curl up.

She sat on a small wooden bench filled with white silk, her knees pressed into a pillow, and her arms crossed over the window sill to steady herself. She was so close to our room's small, singular window that it was almost as if she wanted to fall out of it.
'What?'
'Come and look!' She said her optimum was becoming increasingly addictive.
'Fine,' I said with false irritation.
I placed my arms through my black nightgown and shuffled my feet into the gold-dripped slippers.
'Yes?'
She clapped and pointed to the carriage. I let my eyes examine the procession of blue carriages and horses dressed in white and silver armour.
The soldiers were all carrying boxes and flowers I could get myself. Our wardens had arrived.

Great.

'He is here,' she sang.

'And you are happy about that?'

'Mel,' she shoved me as she sighed, her hand slipping onto her cheek

'Joking,' I said, resting my arms on the stone, 'well, he is rich.'

'He is a King,'

'The King of the Beasts,' I mocked.

The legends of their family were known no matter what kingdom they were from; as powerful as we were as witches, they were equivalent to how dangerous they could become as wolves if angered.

'Mhm,' my sister nodded, either oblivious to my sarcasm or uncaring.

She loved to ignore the reality of their blood; perhaps she truly didn't care; perhaps she enjoyed that all would fear her husband.

'Father is going to let us out today?' I asked, my eyes still analysing the celebrations outside.

'Yes, it was my request, and Besr is almost as powerful as Father; he cannot say no to him.'

'At least one thing good will come out of this,' I muttered.

'Mel, you haven't even met him!'

'I will today; for once we will not be locked in separate rooms. Besides, if his brother has any inclination, he is horrible.

'Dwayne is not that awful,'

'True,' I rolled my eyes, 'but he is annoying. You have not met Dwayne or spent more than a couple of hours with his brother once a year.'

'And that's why I'll spend the entire weekend with him,' she sighed with happiness, and I knew I had lost her to her daydreams.

I frowned looking at my sister. 'I'll miss you,'

She hugged me close. 'I know, but you get a weekend out too. You *did* decline Dwayne's offer for a weekend out.'

'I guess but what will I do without you?'

'Have fun?'

I laughed, 'fun? I think I've forgotten that activity,'

Right at that moment, our guard walked in silent as always. A reminder to begin preparations for our meetings.

Although he was silent, gracefully, he took everyone's attention in each room he entered. Even with his drab black uniform, his brown hair tucked away, and the brown skin that painted him so carefully shining through it all, the sunlight still bounced off his angled cheekbones.

But he remained silent behind us, with his attention certainly not on me.

My sister smiled as she gave a glance at the guard. 'At least you'll have someone to have fun with. Perhaps you will find something to do,'

I groaned, giving her a small hit on the arm. 'Shut up, I whispered.

'Nope.' She looked back at me with a smirk. 'Funny how Father banned everyone from touching us but him.'

'Isn't it?' I whispered with a smile.

Three

Aria

I waited hours for my father to finish his business, hours spent readying myself to be as perfect as possible. It all came down to this; years of tears and letters had led up to this.

A whole weekend with my fiance!

I had grown to love him through the letters we passed since I was old enough to eloquently write. My mother arranged this marriage at my birth, being the true decision-maker before her death. I played with my hair as my mind wondered, What kind of Queen would I become? What kind of wife?

Would I be like my mother, who was strong, powerful, and beautiful to the point of legend, having more power than my father even though she wouldn't be queen without him? Or would I be like my Aunt Talia who lived in the Fae Kingdom, ruling without her husband's opinion and loved by all?

Although we had spent a day together once a year since birth, this would be the first without my father looking and judging our every move.

'Let us leave,' Mel said, taking my hand and running out of the large door made of engraved roses and snowflakes. My mother's two favourite things.

Between the creaky stairs that ran through the tall building were three floors.

The bottom floor consisted of the servant's quarters; we had only seen the large atelier at the bottom of the stairs. I had never attempted to open the old creaky doors that belonged to the servants; one of those rooms must have been a large kitchen to tend to our nutritional needs.

The second floor was much more elegant and graceful; the walls were all white with golden flowers running across as if they were alive. On each door of the building was carved a crescent moon and sun to symbolize the power of our blood. Although there were seven kingdoms, we were by far the most powerful, and my father refused anyone to forget it.

As we stepped outside, the wind tugged at the edges of my gown, lifting the embroidered layers as though even the breeze wanted to celebrate today. The castle loomed ahead, its walls gleaming white in the midday sun, and for a moment, I imagined my mother watching over us, her favourite roses climbing the ancient stone.

I held onto my sister's arm with excitement as we strolled across the field to the main castle with our usual shadows, of course. Kal was following Melody, whereas Nasir was following me.

Nasir was my mother's Page, from the second she entered

this castle, he was never more than five steps behind her till her death, and then he spent his evenings kneeling beside her in tears. He ran to me, offering his arm to make the stroll easier in the heels and extravagant gown I chose for the occasion, which I gladly took. His kind brown eyes always comforted me; he smiled softly as we continued our walk.

My dress was made specifically for this moment; the layers of white and gold ran from my waist. The last layer was almost cream with rows of gold sewn expertly, the embroidery as delicate as glass, transforming me into art.

My sister wore the same dress but refused any embroidery across it and opted for her colours, black and purple. She was to marry Besr's brother, but legends surrounded them.

It was said that they were beasts at night, bears or wolves, or perhaps a hybrid. Each kingdom was once ruled by a Shadow Creature and theirs was once ruled by the Wolves. But the problem was each child would have different abilities from their ancestors; some were only changed by the moon, some at will, some were born red wolves, and some were silver. Who knew what they would be?

But I had *hoped* I would marry into a bloodline that was of witches like us; although I love him, of course, I did, but it would have been nice to have someone who I could mix magic with, learn with, and even fight with.

But we were lucky. That is what Father told us.

Witches were pure magic, and so our bloodline never diluted changed. The sheer power had never been threatened in the centuries we were the High Family.

*** *** ***

'Aria,' the dark roar called out. My face lit up before my eyes ran into his soft blue eyes; he wore a fitted white suit, his blonde mane of curls running into the sky effortlessly. He bowed from the head silently, his eyes never leaving mine.

'Besr,' his name, briefly a whisper of contentment. Nasir took a step away from me with a bow, disappearing into the shadows.

I took a deep breath to prepare my heart as I dipped into a quick curtsy. It was always like this when I saw him. My heart thudded, dropping to my stomach, and my throat was so full of butterflies that words hardly came out of it.

'You are as beautiful as ever,' he said, stepping forward, his hand reaching for mine before he pulled it away. Our eyes locked as I straightened my back, standing a step away from him once again.

'Why thank you, My sister Melody is here.' I pulled my sister towards the men.

'Dwayne?' Besr hit his brother's shoulder.

Dwayne had the same blue eyes and blonde curls as Besr yet was softer in every way. His eyes were warm, whereas Besr's were intense enough to ruin me; his smile was not sly, and his curls were loose and short.

'Yes?' Dwayne stepped forward. 'Hi,' he nodded at us quickly while his eyes seemed distracted.

'Hi,' Mel kept her arms crossed and an enchanting frown on her face; her eyes, although seemingly trying to kill Dwayne, somehow made her even more stunning, almost like a siren.

'Your father said we can take a stroll through the gardens,'

'Really?' I took his hand with both of mine. 'Will you be okay, Mel?' I looked at my sister, trying to decipher her eyes as only I could.

She smiled softly, 'I'll be fine. Do not worry about me; go have fun.'

'Would you-'

'Nope,' she said, finishing Dwayne's sentence.

Dwayne nodded, stepping back from her once again.

* * *

I loved how the heat of the sun always tickled my face, how the smell of the pure air around me was original to this region, with a subtle smell of the thousands of roses in the kingdom, and even how the trees swayed in the wind. I could stare at them for hours.

'I have missed you,' he said, pulling me out of my memorization.

'Thank you, Besr'

'Here,' he said, stopping midst the rows of perfectly cut green grass.

I smiled, taking the small white velvet box. Besr always liked to give me gifts. 'Now what is this?'

'Have a look, my dear,'

I unlatched the small silver lock, opening the box with his family crest across it. A perfect L in blue, I gasped as my eyes took in the sparkles of the necklace.

'Here, allow me to put it on you.'

I stopped as Besr clasped the choker behind my neck; it was made of diamonds with his family's cruel crest hanging in the middle. The thin white ribbon clung to my neck as I played with the crest made of diamonds that hung in the middle; pearls surrounded the letter of their family, a beautiful L.

'It's… exquisite,' I whispered, my fingers brushing the cool diamonds. A small weight settled on my chest as I touched the crest, its sharp edges pressing lightly against my skin. 'Thank you, Besr. It's—' I paused, unsure how to express the mix of gratitude and unease that fluttered in my heart. "It's perfect."

Besr's fingers brushed my skin as he fastened the necklace, and though I smiled, a tiny knot formed in my stomach. His touch was always so deliberate, so precise—like he was performing a task rather than sharing a moment. But I banished the thought from my mind. This was the first weekend we had alone. Surely, I was overthinking.

'Yes, it was my mother's and hers before that,'
    'Thank you,' I beamed as he moved me towards him, his eyes peering into me yet again.
    'Of course, it will grant you the privilege of the world knowing you are my family.'
    With no words coming to mind, I simply nodded and took his hand without Nasir's eyes for once to continue our walk.

Four

Melody

I sat on the small stage filled with pillows and blankets as
Dwayne sat beside me in silence.

Dwayne was not the love of my life. He was beautiful in
that annoyingly angelic way; he was smart, kind, and somewhat
brave. Even in war and weaponry, he was skilled, although he
had never fought.

He also happened to be one of the most irritating men I knew,
and his eyes wandered. One thing was sure about this marriage:
it would not be like my father's.

Dwayne was stunning yet for the life of me, every time he
attempted flirting with me in the past, he ended up in pain.
Unfortunately, kicking and putting your fiance in a headlock
had become undignified as we grew older.

'Where is your mind today?' I asked him.

'What?' He asked, his eyes still staring at the happy couple as
they walked through the garden outside.

'You keep staring at the sky,' I glimpsed out the window to the masterpiece of colours and pastel shades that created our sky, 'your brother?' I eyed Besr with a frown.

'I just do not think she should visit us this weekend,'

'Why? Dwayne...' I looked at him, and although we never had love between us, there was a secret trust there.

He looked at me, his finger keeping his head up as he stayed silent.

'Dwayne!' I hit his arm in a sudden rush of impatience.

He groaned, 'there is a full moon this weekend,' he grumbled, stroking his arm.

'What? But Aria-'

'our ancestor's blood is very diluted now. We hardly ever change unless it is a blood moon,' he rambled.

'A blood moon?'

'Yes, it grants us maximum power and is the only time we can turn others, just as the Immortals.'

'It is not a blood moon this weekend,'

'No.'

'Fine,' I sighed, turning to sit on the pillows laid out for us in the corner.

Dwayne joined me silently.

I raised an eyebrow at him, 'What?'

'I heard that you both have spent your life fighting; your father boasts a very powerful army.'

I nodded, 'Yes.'

'you have many skills,'

'Of course, it grows dull to spend your life in a tower.'

'True...' I realised my slip was too late, 'don't get me wrong, Father does let us out.'

'Yes when it suits him,' he said, rolling his eyes.

'Dwayne?'

'Come on, I have known you all my life, I may not be in love with you, but I do care for you. Why do you never say anything?'

I shrugged as I took a chocolate from the golden plate they had placed in the middle of the stage, surrounding tea and other sweet treats, 'because it is easier, you must pick your battles, it isn't that bad.'

'Whatever,' he whispered, playing with the wrappers on the plate.

* * *

The hours ticked by as I made false excuses to Kal that he didn't believe, forcing me to stay here.

'Do you simply wish to block me of my every goal this weekend?' Dwayne shouted out as he slept among the pillows.

'Whatever do you mean?' I looked over my shoulder as Dwayne sat up from where he was resting.

'Allow us to leave,' Dwayne whined. 'Let us do something,'

'Do you not wish to spend time talking together?' I laughed softly as I watched his eyes squint in annoyance.

'Do you?' He snapped.

'As much as you, I believe,'

'Exactly,' he said, crossing his arms as if he was a toddler.

'Then leave me to my rest, please.'

He frowned, 'This is the only weekend your father has allowed you out without guards and you wish to rest?'

'Perhaps I enjoy my guards' presence,'

'Why? They are just your protectors'

'They are my friends'

He looked at Kal and said back to me, 'That is sad.'

'What is?'

'It is sad that your only friends are servants.'

'Hush,' I threw a pillow at him.

He caught it with a grin. 'Gladly,' he smiled, 'I will go enjoy my guest's company if my work here is done.'

'You brought one of your Concubines?'

'Yes,' he jumped up with style and flair as he always did, 'but she is my only, for once.'

'You do realise if we marry, you are not allowed concubines.'

'Unless you have them too, yes, I know,'

I cocked my head, my forearms resting on the pillows as I looked up to him, 'you wish for me to take a paramour?'

'Yes.'

'Perhaps,' I looked over to Kal as I bit my cheek.

'The only use you will have for me is to bear an heir,' he joked.

"I don't want children."

The words hung in the air, heavier than any of the pillows beneath us. Dwayne blinked, his playful grin faltering. His fingers, once lazily tapping the plate, went still.

"But… your bloodline," he said slowly as if testing the weight of each word.

"I have a sister," I replied, picking up a piece of chocolate and letting it melt against my tongue, its bitterness grounding me as his confusion settled in the space between us.

His fallen face reminded me of my own when I had discovered the truth of my and Aria's birth and the prophecy that came with it.

'You will give your crown to her?'

'Her second born, yes,'

'I have no say in this?' He asked, and his eyes grew wider with every word that left my mouth.

'You may have children,' I stood, taking his hand in mine with a soft smile, 'I will love them as your wife.'

'But not as their mother?'

'No. I never wished to be a mother, Aria did, I only wish to be a great Queen.'

He nodded slowly as my hands left his. 'See you tomorrow,' he sighed, turning on his heel.

'See you then!' I yelled out, falling back into the rows of pillows and silks. I looked out the window, my mind going to the tales I had heard about the brothers—lies and rumours, of course.

My father would never want us to marry someone who had the power to hurt us; he would kill them if there was even a chance. I sighed, looking back at Kal, ignoring the whispers in the back of my mind.

Five

Aria

The journey passed by easily; it was the first time in years I had been in a carriage. Besr opened the window so the breeze could fall on my face as I rested my arms on the window, still smiling as the trees rushed passed me too quickly for me to register fully. Thankfully, one of Besr's many castles was made on the border of our kingdoms.

The kingdom of Fenori was beautiful. Surrounded by nature, it was not like my own home. There were no polished flowers and trimmed hedges; it was simply chaotic and untouched.

As we kept to the stony road, I could see the cruel trees with their frail branches reaching into the sky and the overgrown grass filled with dark shades of green, but perhaps the most beautiful thing of all was the unfiltered streams that ran through the woods.

Besr seemed uninterested as he kept his eyes on his journals, spending the journey working as my dreams of running through the woods grew more and more realistic. After what seemed like hours, the kingdom crept up on us.

His castle was isolated, sitting where his kingdom began. Walls and gates surrounded it. You could not see the nearest town from here, only the forest. I guess it made sense that the nobility would like to run wild in their beastly forms.

He grabbed my waist, letting me jump slightly onto the stone path that led to his home. I grinned as the large gates snapped open, revealing a new world.

The castle was beautiful; the inside smelt of sugar and pure sweetness. My eyes couldn't remove themselves from the dome ceiling, the most beautiful art piece covering it entirely, of blue and white, of course. Flowers and nature stretch across the ceiling. It was a simple design, but it had entrapped me.

He took my lace-covered hand. 'Come,' he ordered.

Rows of servants bowed as we entered, all looking to the floor. They were dressed in blue and white, almost identical, with their eyes hidden and their hair covered.

I began to walk toward them, but he gripped my wrist, his hand surrounding my thin wrist. ' Where are you going?'

'To say hello,' I said, looking up at him with a smile and fake wide eyes.

'I forgot your gentle heart,' he replied, dropping my wrist, 'There is no need; Mr and Mrs Smith are in charge of the staff.'

'Okay but what if I need something?'

'Then you ask them for it; they will assign someone the chore; besides, you will have your choice of ladies-in-waiting once you move here. I already have found a good selection.'

I nodded slowly, 'My stepmother is probably the closest thing I have to one.'

'It is undignified that your father has not allowed you one,' he sucked his teeth, 'I understand his worries but you deserve the privileges of a girl of your stature.'

'I know,'

'Follow me.'

I nodded as he began to run up the stairs. As we reached the second floor, he took my hand in his. Our fingers intertwined completely.

I gasped, 'Careful,'

'There are no eyes now; in my kingdom, we can find small gaps in your father's rules,' he whispered, with a hint of a demon in his eyes.

His hand slid around my waist with ease, as if he owned the right to touch me. A part of me was thrilled at his nearness, at the warmth of his fingers on my skin. But another part, a quieter voice at the back of my mind, whispered that this wasn't freedom. This was something else entirely. I wasn't so sure I even enjoyed his touch; rather just being touched.

He laughed as he pulled himself away, leaping higher and higher through the stairs, forcing me to chase him—almost so fast I fell.

'Close your eyes' he whispered.

I smiled, letting myself plunge into darkness as he walked up the last step and steadily towards a new room. I heard the doors clang open and drifted to the subtle smell of lilies and violets.

'Open them,'

I gasped; he had included me in the room. Touches of me were midst the pale blue and snow-white room. Books hidden on a shelf, brushes and a canvas tucked into a corner, and lilies in vases across the room.

I walked into my room and said, "It is beautiful, thank you," looking back at him as he stood to the side, watching my face and analysing me.

'I want to make our room feel perfect for you,' he said, staying a step behind me as I walked further into the room.

'I am glad,' my fingers traced the embroidery on the bed filled with silks and pillows, i looked over my shoulder, 'but we cannot sleep in the same bed just yet.'

'We would not want your father to kill me,'

'That would be poor,' I chuckled.

'Very,' he laughed, shutting the door, 'I will let you change, I have planned a dinner for us to get to know each other, really get to know each other.'

I beamed, 'Thank you,' I said, turning to him.

He took out a golden heart-shaped key from his chest pocket as he began to walk to the door.

My heart dropped as my hand raised to him before realising, 'Wait, Besr.'

'Yes?'

'What are you doing?' I asked him as I raced to the door.

He sighed, holding up the key. 'Sorry, my love but I have to.'

'Why?'

'I agreed with your father; it is just too dangerous.'

'Why?' I cried.

"Your father has told me of your ability and your *curse*."

The word stung. *Curse*. He spoke of it like it was a foregone conclusion, a flaw etched into my very blood. But we didn't even know if I bore it. None of us did.

"We don't even know if it's me," I snapped, the frustration bubbling to the surface.

He sighed, and for a brief moment, I thought I saw something like regret in his eyes. But it was gone as quickly as it came.

"Better safe than sorry, my love," he whispered, his voice soft but unyielding.

I stood frozen in the centre of the room. A prison. Not of stone walls and towers this time, but of promises and treaties, of expectations and gentle hands. I had always thought that marriage was freedom, a way to escape Father's shadow.

I sighed 'I am not; I understand,' I slumped my shoulders as I knew like my father, his mind was not to be changed.

'I do not wish for your father to hate me any more than he does.'

'Are you scared of him?'

'Of course I am. He is the Mad King after all,'

'Fine,' I said with my arms folded, 'but when we marry, I will not be locked into a room.'

'I know it was written into the treaty of our union.'

'Good,' I said, my arms returning to my side.

He kissed my cheek softly, his fingers gripping my chin. I gasped, my eyes staying on the floor while a small smile crept onto my lips.

'Now rest,' he hesitated for a mere second before turning away from me.

'Mhm,' I said, crossing my arms as he slipped behind the white door. As the click of the lock echoed in the room, a cold shiver ran down my spine. I wanted to believe Besr, to trust that he was only acting out of concern. But his words lingered in my mind like a shadow. Dangerous for whom? My hands trembled as I crossed my arms, and for the first time, I wondered if Melody had been right all along. Was I just trading one prison for another? But as I stared at the locked door, a new fear unfurled in my chest. What if this was only the beginning?

* * *

I pressed the soft pink blush onto my cheeks, staring into the mirror as anticipation twisted and fluttered in my stomach. The door would open any moment now. My reflection stared back, softer than I usually saw myself—not the kind of beauty that echoed my mother's regal elegance, but something simpler, something distinctly mine. I let my hair cascade over my shoulders, the silky locks brushing against the lightweight pink dress that swayed with every small movement. It wasn't ornate or bejewelled, just a simple flow of fabric that felt as free as the breeze on a spring morning.

The faint creak of the door made my heart leap. Besr's reflection filled the tall and steady mirror, his presence a calm that somehow ignited chaos within me. His hands settled on my shoulders, warm and grounding, and the butterflies in my chest stirred with life.

'Ready, my queen?' His voice was as smooth as the fabric I wore, yet carried the weight of something much deeper.

I nodded, slipping my hand into his as he helped me. His other hand settled gently against my lower back, guiding me out of the room. The simple gesture, so natural yet intimate, made me smile to myself.

The dining room was quiet, save for the soft rustle of fabric and the sound of our steps. At the centre stood a small table, set for two, with chairs positioned to face one another. He pulled one out for me with an effortless grace, his fingers brushing mine as he helped me sit. My gloved hands tingled where his touch lingered.

The table was modest—two plates of rice and meat, and a single silver goblet resting between us. I tilted my head, a curious smile tugging at my lips.

'What's this?' I asked, trying to suppress the amusement in my tone.

Besr chuckled; his voice was rich with pride. 'I had the cook teach me a simple meal.'

'You… cooked?' I blinked, glancing at the plate before meeting his eyes again. 'For *me?*'

'Of course.' His laughter was soft, and the way his gaze lingered on me made my cheeks flush. He took my hand in his, his thumb brushing over the silk of my glove before he lifted it to his lips. The kiss was brief but reverent, sending a warmth through me.

With a practiced motion, he reached for the goblet and poured a rich, dark cherry juice into my glass. 'Now,' he said, his tone shifting to something softer, more curious, 'tell me everything about the prophecy.'

Six

Melody

I stared at Kal from my bed, flipping through the large book left for me. I tilted my head until he looked back at me.

'Someday I will make you laugh,' I drew my knees, my light layered lilac dress covering me entirely, to my chest, placing the book softly by me.

'Mhm,' Kal answered, his posture unchanged as he stood in front of my door. He wore his hair up today; it suited him; his small, angular face was more on display, and his eyes were soft and bored. Instead of his usual uniform, he wore a white soft suit, the gold scarf of his uniform running down his right shoulder, trapped with his belt as usual. At least he kept the symbol that I owned him.

'You know, you are the only guard that does not speak to me.'

'yes.'

I threw a pillow at the wall, but of course, his face did not even flinch. 'I'll jump out the window.'

'You do that.'

'I'm serious. In my undergarments.'

Kal's lips twitched—just for a second, but enough to make me pause. 'Your father would love that,' he said, a ghost of a smile hidden beneath his words.

'I am going to leave the tower in nothing but my undergarments!'

I stared at his face, waiting for a reaction. 'You are painstakingly relaxed,'

'Yes.'

Where the fuck was he going tonight?

'Great,' I sighed, falling back into my bed, my hair falling softly across the pillows.

'Are you ready for Dwayne?'

Why was he so adamant about me leaving him? Did he have somewhere to be? Could I keep him with me?

I groaned, 'Must you remind me?'

'He has been waiting outside the door for thirty minutes now.'

'Why is he allowed inside the tower?' I asked as I slipped into my black boots.

'He is your fiance; your sister has travelled to her fiance's castle.'

'At least she gets a weekend out,'

'You get to go to the gardens,'

'*Great.*'

'Hurry.'

I jumped out of bed with a sad sight, exaggerating each second of it.

'Fine just for you,' I teased with a small wink as he opened the door. 'Wanna come with?' I asked him with my arms behind my back and a soft tilt of my head, allowing my hair to sway in the wind as I passed him.

'Not particularly.'

'Rude.'

As Kal turned away with his usual indifference, I felt a small pang of something sharp and bitter. I hid it, of course, behind a smile and a wink, as I always did. But deep down, the realization gnawed at me: even here, surrounded by people, I was alone.

* * *

Dwayne was used to my informal appearance; he was one of the only people who would never comment on my experiments with hair or if I did not wish to wear the most beautiful gown. It was a small comfort, I guess, to know he was perfectly content with me.

'I will return home today,' he told me after mere moments of our stroll through the garden.

'So soon?' I asked as we walked, removing my arm from his as we stood in the middle of the many gardens of my home. Surrounded were my mother's ruby-red roses, which she loved to plant. The sweet smell was my favourite reminder of her.

'It is boring here,'

'I am sure,'

'And I miss my home.'

'You mean your Concubines,' I whispered, looking back at my guards who stayed under the rose trees my mother loved dearly, one of the white roses and the other red.

He rolled his eyes with a smirk, 'till next time.'

'Til next time, tell Aria hi.'

'I will do,'

I watched him jog off, disappearing between the rosebushes like a fleeting memory. Part of me was relieved—Dwayne's presence was a constant reminder of a future I never asked for. But another part, a smaller part, wondered if I would ever get used to the way people left so easily. As Dwayne walked away, my eyes drifted to the edge of the garden, where the trees met the sky in a wild blur of green and gold. I wanted to run—to chase after the wind, to lose myself in something beyond these walls. But I stayed, rooted to the ground like one of my mother's roses, beautiful and trapped.

Seven

Aria

❧

'Where are we going, Besr?'

I called out as I followed him down the hall, clutching my skirts so I could keep up with his pace.

'Hurry.'

We reached our destination as Besr led me to two large doors, painted white with a large gold A, written with swirls and soft elegance.

I gasped, letting go of my skirts so they fell around my ankles.

The guards opened the doors to the great room, the walls replaced by mirrors, the ceilings filled with paintings of stories. I laughed, spinning to view every inch of the masterpiece within the room. I paused as the eagle eyes of someone I knew from memories of my childhood lessons appeared.

King Resi, the first-born half-born of the wolves, was the first king of Fenori. It was said he was exactly his nature—in the light the most charming, handsome, saintly man but in the shadows, the animal that lived within him came out to play. I found myself walking towards his large portrait, as always he was dressed in white and blue, forcing his ice-cold eyes to seem even brighter.

It was clear Besr was his direct descendant.

I heard the doors clang once again, forcing me to turn around. Only then did I realise the room was empty except for a table filled with every shade of paint, of every colour you could think of, a matching chair, and a large canvas.

'Forgive me,' he called out as he entered the room.

'Thi-this is beautiful,' I said as I walked further into the room, forgetting he was even there. My eyes taking in every beautiful detail of the room. Paintings of women with *my* necklace were hung. Without noticing, I touched the soft L that swung from my neck.

'I knew you would love it, I had it polished, every spec for you to enjoy your time here, this is the Queen's room, my mother has already passed; you can use it now.'

I turned to him immediately, 'You will allow me to spend my time here? Alone?'

'That is why I chose your room; there is a short, secluded hallway that goes from your room straight to here,' he said, strolling towards me as my eyes couldn't take in all of the beauty.

'Thank you,' I said, taking his hand in mine, staring into his eyes Even this small gesture was as intimate as we could be.

'Always, my love. We may fight, but I do love you. You see that. I will always love you and protect you.'

'Of course,' I replied, but the word caught in my throat. His icy eyes held me in place, but somewhere deep inside, uncertainty stirred. Did I truly believe him? Or was I too afraid to ask the lingering questions in the shadows?

'We have the next day together before you must go home.'

'Yes, we are lucky the borders are so close.'

'Yes, but I cannot wait till you can stay here forever with me.' He grinned so magnificently that it was all I needed—almost to forget my worries.

'Mhm,' I nodded as I gazed across the promise of a life I wished to live.

Forever… that word repeated itself in a million different ways.

Forever seems almost a vow.

Forever.

* * *

'What is that racket?' I tore off my sleeping mask and ripped the covers aside. The sound of shouting—guards mixed with guttural roars—shattered the stillness.

'Besr,' I called out, heart hammering in my chest.

Before I could rise, Nasir burst into the room, wearing my family's gold crest across his chest. His expression was grim. 'My lady, you must stay in your chambers,' he said, gripping my wrist gently.

I threw off his hand, sliding out of bed. 'Careful, Nasir. My father and fiancé would kill you for touching me without cause.'

'They'd kill me for less,' he muttered, 'but this is about your *safety*. Come.'

'What is happening?' I demanded, shoving my feet into golden slippers. The cold air pricked at my bare arms, and I hesitated to step out in just my light nightgown.

'There's a rabid beast loose,' he said grimly.

'A *what?*'

'No time to explain.' He pulled me behind him as we moved into the dim hallway, his shield and sword already drawn. The chill of the stone floors seeped through my slippers, and the flickering light of torches painted shadows on the walls. Then I saw it—a massive silhouette skittering in the dark. My breath hitched as the sound of claws on stone sent shivers down my spine.

A guttural growl rumbled through the air.

'Aria!'

I whirled around. 'Dwayne?' Relief briefly warmed my chest as he stumbled into view, his hair dishevelled and his new-found rose-coloured eyes wide with panic.

'Stay calm,' he said, his words shaky as his hands flailed uselessly. 'It's Besr.'

'What?' The relief evaporated. 'You said you hardly ever change!'

'Hardly! Keyword, hardly!' He said, waving his hands as if that explained everything. 'There are exceptions!'

'This is the exception?'

'Yes!' Dwayne nodded frantically, his voice rising to a whine. 'Look, he won't change back until he either *strikes someone* or the moon sets.'

My stomach sank. 'Strikes someone? What are you talking about?'

'Our wolf blood is diluted, but violence triggers humanity. If he attacks someone, it should force him to shift back,' Dwayne stammered.

'Great,' Nasir muttered, stepping in front of me with his sword raised.

Before anyone could respond, Besr's low growl reverberated again, closer this time. His white-furred form crept into the light, eyes gleaming and nostrils flaring as he fixed his gaze on us.

Dwayne yelped and shoved me forward. 'Hit *her*, not me!'

Nasir didn't even spare him a glance. 'This is who Mel is marrying?' he asked, deadpan.

Besr lunged. A massive paw swiped through the air, and Dwayne's scream tore through the corridor as he crumpled to the ground, clutching his chest. Blood bloomed across his white shirt, spreading like split wine.

'Dwayne!' I shouted, rushing forward, but Nasir pulled me back.

'I'm fine,' Dwayne whimpered, his voice strained. 'Just bleeding...to death."

Besr frozen mid-step. His claws twitched, and the fur on his arms began to shed in patches. A sickening crack filled the space as his bones shifted, forcing him back into his human form. The growl in his throat turned into a guttural groan, and he staggered forward on bare feet.

'Aria,' he rasped, his voice hoarse as his hands found my waist. His gaze, no longer wild, locked on mine. 'I didn't harm you, did I?'

I shook my head, heart pounding. 'No, Besr. You didn't.'

'But you harmed *me*,' Dwayne groaned from the floor, gesturing at the blood seeping through his torn shirt.

'Nasir?' I called out.

'I've got him.' Nasir crouched beside Dwayne, slipping an

arm under his shoulders to hoist him up.

'Better you than her,' Besr muttered, brushing a stray curl from my face.

Dwayne shot him a withering glare. 'I'm your *blood!*'

'And?' Besr said, barely sparing him a glance.

With a scowl, Dwayne leaned heavily on Nasir, his steps slow and uneven as they made their way down the hall. 'Unbelievable,' he muttered under his breath.

I sighed, leaning back into Besr's steadying hands. 'We're going to have to explain this to my father.'

Besr smirked, his gaze softening as his fingers brushed against mine. 'We'll figure it out.'

For now, the air was still, save for the distant echo of Dwayne's muttered complaints.

Eight

Melody

Aria trembled as Father paced the room, his hands clenched tightly behind his back. His brown eyes, usually warm, had darkened with a storm of anger. I recognized the stance immediately—the rigid posture, the hands gripping each other behind his back. I'd learned years ago that this was the moment to leave. But this time, his anger was well-justified.

'I refuse to marry a coward, Father,' I said, injecting a note of defiance into my voice. This was the perfect opportunity to dodge marriage. Yes, I was furious that Dwayne had endangered Aria, but perhaps now Father would let me go. He may want me engaged, but surely not to someone who would sacrifice my sister.

Father's face twisted. 'Yes, I have half a mind to kill them both with my bare hands.'

Aria shot to her feet. 'You will not!' she yelled, surprising even me. The one time she stands up to him, and it's for *him*? My stomach twisted.

I forced a laugh. 'Fine, kill Dwayne, then. I don't mind.' I joked.

Aria glared at me, her voice a whine. 'He's my fiance's brother.'

'Fine,' I replied, shrugging. 'Then at least cancel *my* engagement.'

Father's mouth opened, ready to launch into one of his lectures about my mother's wishes. 'Your mother wanted—'

'She wanted us united,' I interrupted. 'Aria's marriage will accomplish that.'

He groaned, pinching the bridge of his nose. 'Why choose now to do this, Mel?'

'Because before, we only saw each other once a year. It was a chore. But now...' I glanced at Aria, who nodded, picking up the thought.

'Now it's happening,' she finished softly.
    'Exactly, and this is the perfect excuse; Arias' engagement will not be threatened,' I took Father's hands into mine, looking upon him with as soft a look I could muster. 'Please Father, I accept your every decree; work hard and do everything I can to be the best daughter I can be. Please grant me this request,'

'Fine,' my father placed his hand in the sky in defeat.

'Mel, are you sure? Don't you want to be free?' Arias's eyes searched mine, her fingers clutching on my shoulders.

'I refuse to trade one prison for another.'

'It would not be a prison,'

'It will be for me, you have something with Besr I will never have with Dwayne.'

She dropped my hands and nodded with her eyes on the floor, 'Fine.'

'I will need to speak to Nasir; perhaps he is getting too old for this job.'

'you cannot fire him,' I pleaded to my father, ' he was mother's best friend, he held her hand through her pregnancy, through becoming high-queen, he watched us grow up.'

Aria bit her cheek, 'Father, please.'

His hesitation grew too long.

That was all she said, her quiet plea, I looked back at him and said, 'You cannot do this; i will not allow it!'

'do not tell me what to do!'

Aria hugged my father close, 'Of course, father, but I beg of you, do not take away one of our dearest friends; he is family. Mother used to tell us to call him Uncle.'

He nodded, 'Fine, but he can no longer be the only one to watch over you, Aria; Kal will have to find a soldier to attend to you both when you visit Besr.'

'thank you, Father,'

I swallowed my rage, 'thank you.'

* * *

'Mel,'

'Yes?'

'You know better than to tell Father what to do; it bruises his ego.'

I nodded, sighing. 'I know. I just got—'

'Angry?'

'Yeah. How do you *not*?'

A slow breath left her lips, the kind that felt heavy with years of secrets and swallowed words. 'I do. But sometimes you have to know when to hold your tongue. Father wouldn't *truly* hurt Nasir—he's a reminder of Mother.'

'Yeah, but—'

'But nothing.' She yelled. She sighed, 'Mel, he would have hurt him just to prove he could. He loves that power.' She said softly.

I looked away, my hands clenched tightly at my sides. 'Doesn't that make you angry?'

'Of course it does. It makes me feel small and voiceless. But he's still our father, Mel. He loves us, in his way. We just… have to learn when to toe the line.'

I scoffed, bitterness slipping into my voice. 'When did you get so wise?'

She smiled faintly, a sad, knowing twist of her lips. 'After watching you. I learn a lot from your mistakes. Observing is a form of survival.'

'I hate observing,' I muttered, glancing down at the floor.

Her fingers touched my shoulder, gentle but firm. 'I know.'

Nine

Aria

∞

'Father, Mel,' I nodded at them both as I walked towards them. The palace sitting behind them, majestically against the sky, a fortress of stone and marble crowned with dark, glistening spires. Ivy clung to the lower walls, softening the harshness of the grey stone while towering, arched windows gleamed with the reflection of the sun. Ornate balconies jutted out at intervals, framed by intricate carvings of mythical beasts, and banners bearing the royal crest fluttered in the breeze. Surrounded by lush gardens and guarded by a high, wrought-iron fence, the palace was both beautiful and imposing—a place of elegance and quiet menace, as unyielding as the royalty who lived within.

My father wore a smile I never had the pleasure of being the cause of, as he and Mel talked.

'I cannot believe you get to leave tonight and spend the entire day out without guards,' Mel laughed.

'Why else get engaged?' I whispered with a devilish smile to Mel.

'Aria,' my father frowned.

I sighed, my eyes falling to the floor, 'I am joking, Father,' I whispered.

'Whatever will I do?' Mel sighed dramatically, placing her hand on her forehead and she swooned.

'Play cards by yourself,' I teased before walking backwards with a laugh to the carriage as she stood with a frown.

Kal held my hand as he helped me into the large carriage, Besr leaned forward with my oh-so-favourite grin in the world. Nasir followed me in closely behind me.

'Hello, darling,'

'Hello,' I replied as I took my seat.

A kiss was so tempting as we drove out of my father's sight, but were not married yet.

As the carriage made its way out of the golden gates, we entered the town. The town was vibrant and noisy, filled with citizens who waved and cheered as the carriage rolled past. Market stalls lined the streets, their colourful canopies flapping in the breeze, and young girls threw roses at the wheels, their laughter rising like bells.

I loved my people dearly, with the young girls playing in the corner and the screaming babes held by their mothers. I smiled to myself.

'what are you thinking about?' Besr asked.

'our life, our future,'

He followed my eyes, 'You will be a great mother.' He took my knuckle, kissing it softly.

I looked over to see Nasir looking out the other window, his eyes *not* on me.

'I am excited to meet your people; I always wished to know mine more intimately.'

'no need for that, my love; it is what dukes and nobles are for.'

'what do you mean?'

'just that you will have more responsibilities, the court at the main palace will be the people you must look after,'

I nodded slowly as the happy people faded away, replaced by only buildings and then the wild woods. I had forgotten how different our cultures, courts and traditions were, his world was similar to the Fae rather than my own. More rigid, and traditional, as if the centuries had not turned since the Shadow Creatures' ruled.

* * *

'Why are we stopping?' I asked as the carriage screeched to a halt.

'I am sorry, my dear I have some business to tend to but I want you to visit the town, I thought you would enjoy some time by yourself.'

'Okay,'

'do not leave the carriage; just watch over the people,' he said as the door opened and he left me with a slam.

I stared outside at the open blue skies as I waited for our final destination.

'Wha-what's that? I asked Ismal, the only guard that remained on this trip, sitting up as a large building finally came into view. The walls were almost grey, although it seemed to be the height of luxury once, it was simply derelict now.

'Princess, you cannot get out of the carriage; the king and your father will kill me,' he begged.

'I will never allow that; just what is that place? Those children look so unhappy,'

'That is the orphanage.'

'Why is it so derelict?' I looked back at him, 'Surely the royal family takes care of their orphans.'

'I cannot comment on that,'

'Besr is rich beyond compare; I do not understand.'

'It is the way of the land, of the royal family,'

I opened the door before he could stop me. 'Forgive me,' I said as I stepped down, rushing to the gates before the Ismal could catch me.

It smelled rancid as I passed by the ancient bricks, overgrown with ivy. I strolled through the empty garden; a cracked fountain filled with brown water was the only decoration.

Nasir caught up to me as I reached the shut door of the building.

'Please Aria,'

I looked back to his wide brown eyes and trembling hands. 'Just for you,' I told him as I picked up my skirts and walked back with him.

* * *

The carriage door opened, and Besr climbed back in, his face set in an expression of mild boredom as he scanned a parchment in his hands. I watched him for a moment, searching for some spark of empathy, but his gaze was cold, indifferent.

'Why is the orphanage in your town like that?' I asked, the image of those sad children still fresh in my mind.

'Like what?' he replied, barely looking up.

'Unlivable!' I threw my hands up in frustration. 'The walls are crumbling, the garden is dead, and the children—' My voice choked, and I forced myself to calm down. 'They looked so unhappy.'

He looked up finally, his eyes narrowing. 'Do not raise your voice to me like that.'

I bit my lip, forcing my gaze downward. 'I'm sorry. I lost my temper. But… it's important. It was my mother's legacy, to care for our people. Surely, we can do something.'

Besr let out a small, exasperated sigh. 'Perhaps in *your* kingdom, but here it is unimportant.'

My chest tightened as his words sank in. 'Please,' I whispered. 'Allow it to be my project. I can restore the orphanage—I'll handle the work myself, I promise.'

He snorted, folding his parchment. 'You'll have plenty of work to do as my Queen, as my wife. When we're married, you'll join the other ladies of the house. Let the dukes and nobles do this.'

'The other ladies?' A chill ran down my spine. 'What other ladies?'

He waved a dismissive hand. 'The wives of noblemen, visiting court… and, of course, my mistresses.'

'*Mistresses?*' The word felt like a slap, and I turned to Ismal, hoping for a sign that I'd misheard. But his eyes were fixed firmly on the window, his expression impassive

'Yes,' he said as if discussing the weather. 'It is the norm here. You'll have to get used to it.'

'Not for me!' I snapped, pulling my hand away as he tried to reach for it. 'If you have concubines, then so shall I.'

He laughed, a low, mocking sound. 'You will not. In my home, the Queen does not keep concubines. Imagine if you had a child and tried to claim it as legitimate.'

'And what if *you* have a child with one of your mistresses?' I demanded, my voice trembling. 'What if *he* claims the throne?'

He leaned back, smirking. 'The royal blood runs through me. *My* choice will be respected. And as for the throne… your sister's children will inherit, not yours. Don't get any ideas, Aria.'

I chuckled, '*My* child will be Melody's heir, the high- king or queen.'

'And I will forbid it if it is not also my child. I am the King, Aria, and Melody will not be Queen for a *long* time."

I felt my hands ball into fists, my entire body tense with a mixture of anger and despair. Nasir glanced back at me, his hand twitching over his sword hilt, but I shook my head, barely managing to keep my composure.

'How quickly your behaviour changes,' I said, my voice cold and steady. 'Do not forget—we're merely *engaged*. This marriage can still be undone.'

Besr's smile faded, and he leaned forward, his gaze sharp. 'If you break our engagement, your sister's alliance will fall apart as well. You have no choice now.'

He gave me one last, smug look before returning his attention to his papers, dismissing me as if I were nothing more than a piece of art, and I could feel the ice begging to be released from within me. I smiled silently, imagining the view of that frozen smug smirk.

* * *

The knock was soft, almost hesitant.

I didn't need to turn around to know it was him. I could feel his presence as clearly as if he'd already stepped into the room—heavy with regret, yet stubbornly unyielding.

For a moment, I thought about ignoring it, letting him stand there with his guilt and his silence. But what would that accomplish? This wasn't a battle to win, not really, though it had felt like one earlier.

'Come in,' I said, my voice sharper than I meant it to be.

The door opened, the lock clicking open, and there he was.

He always seemed to take up more space than he should—broad shoulders, confident posture—but tonight there was a softness in his eyes that I wasn't used to. Draped over his arm was a dress. Sapphire blue, threaded with silver, it shimmered faintly in the low light.

He held it up slightly, almost like an offering. 'I brought this for you,' he said, his voice careful, cautious. 'And… I wanted to apologize.'

I didn't move. My arms stayed crossed tightly over my chest, a shield against the storm of emotions his presence always seemed to stir in me.

'This,' he said, gesturing to the dress, 'this is what my parents used to do. They believed gestures like this solved everything.' He let out a short, hollow laugh, the sound barely filling the space between us. 'But I realize now it's not enough.'

I raised an eyebrow, watching him carefully. 'No,' I said flatly. 'It's not.'

He flinched, just slightly, but I saw it. Good. Let him feel it. Let him sit in that discomfort for a while.

He stepped closer, and I fought the instinct to take a step back. I wouldn't give him the satisfaction of retreat.

'It's not disrespect, you know,' he said, his voice firmer now. 'Those people—the courtiers, the women—they're your subordinates, yes, but also your friends. And you…' He reached out, hesitating for a moment before his hand brushed my arm. 'You are the Queen. My best friend. My confidant. My *partner*.'

I didn't pull away, but I didn't soften either. My voice came out sharper than I intended. 'Then why were you so angry?'

He sighed, the sound heavy and full of frustration—though I couldn't tell if it was directed at me or himself. 'I'm not used to being questioned, my parents died too early to teach me anything, except how to rule.' he admitted, his words slow, deliberate. 'I'm not used to… this. Being in a relationship.'

That made me turn, my gaze snapping to his. 'We've been in a relationship for years,' I said, each word pointed and precise.

'Yes, I know, my darling.' His lips quirked into a rueful smile, though there was no humour in it. 'But we've spent most of that time apart, talking through surface-level letters. Avoiding the harder conversations. We've never had this depth before.' He gestured between us, his hand cutting through the air as if trying to define something invisible. 'Not like now.'

I didn't respond immediately. Instead, I let myself really look at him—the man who was supposed to be my partner, my equal, and yet who so often seemed unreachable. But not tonight. Tonight, his walls were down, and for the first time in a long time, I could see him.

'And now?' I asked quietly.

'Now…' He straightened, his eyes meeting mine with a steady intensity that made my heart ache. 'Now, we argued. But that's what people do. We'll compromise, we'll discuss—whatever it takes.' His voice broke slightly, the faintest crack in his composure. 'Just don't leave. Stay with me, and we'll figure this out together.'

The vulnerability in his words was like a knife, cutting through my defences in a way I hadn't expected. I wanted to stay angry, to hold onto that righteous indignation, but instead, I felt the edges of my resolve begin to soften.

'Okay,' I said finally, the word almost a whisper.

'Okay?' he repeated, his voice tinged with hope.

I nodded, a faint smile tugging at the corners of my lips despite myself. 'Mhm. I agreed, didn't I?'

Relief flooded his face, and for a moment, we simply stood

there, the tension between us melting away like frost under the sun. He reached for my hand, his thumb brushing over my gloved knuckles in a gesture that felt both tentative and certain.

'We'll figure this out,' he said again as if saying it aloud might make it real.

And as I looked at him, I realized that for all his flaws and all our arguments, I wanted to believe him.

Ten

Melody

I walked into the hallway, checking my skirt and hair before I saw Kal. I ran to him, 'Why have I been summoned so suddenly?'

'Your father is calling for you.'

My heart skipped. 'Why?' I asked instantly, but dread was already creeping in, my mind spinning with scenarios—none of them real, but all of them terrifying.

Kal glanced away, his voice dropping to a whisper. 'He's in a bad mood.'

'Why?' I repeated, gripping her arm. 'Kal, what did I do?'

He sighed. 'I don't know. He's hearing rumours about you.'

'Rumours? About what?' I swallowed, trying to keep my voice steady.

'Just… be careful,' he said, glancing down the hall before leading me toward the grand dining room. I straightened my dress and took a deep breath, forcing myself to walk as if I weren't about to step into a lion's den.

As we entered, my father sat silently, sawing at his food with jerky, irritated movements. His fork screeched against the plate, his muttered curses undercutting the soft click of silverware. I cleared my throat.

'Father?' I asked, my voice almost like air with how soft the word came out of my mouth.

He placed his knife down with a sigh, then raised his goblet to his lips, gulping down cherry-red wine. 'Have you left the tower, my child?'

I froze. The truth sat on the tip of my tongue, but something in his eyes stopped me cold. *He doesn't believe you*, a voice whispered in my mind. *No matter what you say.*

'Answer me!' he barked.

'No, Father,' I managed, my voice small.

He slammed the goblet down, splashing wine across the table. 'Liar.'

My pulse thundered, and I glanced back at Kal. He gave me a small nod, the barest encouragement. I took a shaky step forward. 'No, I-I swear, I haven't—'

'Then promise me on your mother's soul.'

The words stung, sharp as a blade. 'I… I promise.'

'Good girl.' He nodded to himself, picking up his cutlery again, his tone now casual—as if he hadn't just accused me of betrayal. 'I'll find out where this false information came from. I know you would never break the rules.'

For a second, I almost laughed. I couldn't tell him I'd wanted to break the rules and that the idea of leaving this gilded cage was one of the few things that kept me sane. But instead, I nodded, swallowing my words along with my pride.

'Of course not,' I murmured, my gaze dropping to the floor. My mind screamed with a thousand things I wanted to say, but I bit my lip, willing myself to stay silent.

'Don't be angry with me, Mel. I'm doing this to keep you safe; you understand that, don't you? The curse…'

'Yes, Father.' *The curse, the curse.* He reminded me of it every time I dared ask for freedom.

He took another long sip of wine, his gaze drifting back to me.

'You can leave the tower tomorrow; I shall allow you an hour to practice your magic. Your Aunt has been asking for a visit; no doubt she will want to test your capabilities.'

I nodded absent-mindlessly.

'Your elemental power has not come in yet.'

'No, it has not,'

'Your mother's family was infamous for their specialities, but the royal bloodline is known for their elemental magic; you cannot take the throne without it. Powers of the moon or the sun—perhaps you will even inherit one not seen before. You two are the result of two of the most powerful bloodlines in this world.'

'I know, Father,' I sighed quietly; he was too wrapped up in his world to notice, thankfully.

'Good, there is speak of favour for Aria, I love Aria but if she is to be the queen of that beastly kingdom, she cannot also rule ours.'

'I know.'

'And you are the one who has been prepared for this since birth.'

'I know,' my jaw tightened as I spit out the words.

'Just because she is seen as a good princess does not mean she will be a good queen.'

Mhm,' I murmured, half-listening. *I'd lost him again.* When he began his lectures, it was like I wasn't even a person—just an audience for him to project his views onto. Once upon a time, the comparison to Aria would have caused my silent tears to fall, but once you hear about your utter disappointment enough times, it loses meaning. I would get my powers; the prophecy promised that me and my sister would be the most powerful creatures in this world.

'Maybe you should talk more formally like your sister, spend more time with the orphans, dress in less-'

I raised an eyebrow as I dared him to finish his sentence.

I knew he hated how I dressed and how I didn't care for the

finest things in the world. I know he stopped seeing me as his beautiful princess the day I dared to have an opinion.

'Just make sure there is no reason for civil war; do you have any failings?'

'No.'

'Good, good. If needed, you can spend more time working; make sure you are working hard.'

'I am.'

'Good, good, are you even listening?'

'Of course I am.'

'Then stop saying okay, yes,'

'What else am I meant to say?' I bit my cheek; fuck, the words travelled from my mind to my tongue much too quickly.

'You are just mindlessly nodding your head,'

'I agree with you!' My father's anger was racing through me, but unlike my father, I had to tame the unfiltered rage.

'listen!'

'I am! You are very sensitive for someone who hates emotion,' I mumbled.

'What did you say to me?'

'I say one word wrong one phrasing and you do not speak me for days.'

'I have allowed you out of the tower,'

'To have dinner and impress the nobles tonight! Or to yell at me!'

'Guards! Escort Melody back to the tower,'

'Father! You *promised*-'

'You did not get engaged! You still must be protected until you find your great love.'

I scoffed, 'Fine, but an engagement does not mean love; you should know that better than anybody. How is my lovely stepmother, by the way?'

My father scowled as the guards approached me. 'I will walk, thank you,' I said as I returned to my lovely tower.

Eleven

Aria

The storm clouds rolled over the darkened sky like an unspoken omen, casting the forest in a shimmering veil of rain. Inside the grand stone hall of the werewolf king's mountain keep, I stood near the arched window. The rain's rhythmic thuds against the castle walls was a melody only I seemed to hear.

'The rain is pure magic,' I murmured, 'Days like these feel perfect for painting and reflection. Don't you think?'

On the opposite side of the room, leaned against his carved oak throne. His eyes, sharp as a hunter's blade, flicked toward the window but held no trace of her reverence. His brow furrowed, a grimace tugging at his lips.

'Reflection?' he echoed, his deep voice carrying a growl beneath its surface. 'Rain turns the world into a mess. It ruins plans.'

I turned from the window, my iridescent gown shimmering

like starlight, a frown shadowing her delicate features. 'Oh,' I said softly, her sapphire eyes dimming like a candle under a gust. 'I suppose it's just a matter of perspective.'

Besr's claws tapped against the throne's armrest. 'My perspective,' he growled, 'is that we were meant to hunt today, to feel the earth beneath our feet and the thrill of the chase. Instead, we're trapped in here, doing *nothing*.' He walked down the steps and took a seat, I followed suit so we sat beside each other in the red oak chairs.

'Doing nothing? I thought…' my voice wavered, then steadied. 'I thought spending time together, regardless of where we are, was what mattered.'

Besr's lips twitched, almost into a smirk. 'Together, staring out a window?' he said, his tone dry. 'This is wasting the day.'

Wasting? The word echoed in my chest, and my wings of thought clipped mid-flight. She breathed deeply, smoothing her expression into something serene. 'Perhaps you're not as attuned to quiet moments as I'd hoped,' I replied gently.

He sighed, 'I am sorry, I just find it difficult to sit still.'

I nodded, 'I understand.'

The tension in the room was interrupted by the arrival of a servant, who placed a silver tray of pastries on the low table. Besr reached out without a word, taking the largest and sinking his teeth into it.

I blinked, startled. 'I was going to ask if you wanted to share—'

Besr, already mid-bite, glanced at me with a casual shrug. 'You can have the other one.'

My lips pressed together, but I forced a light laugh. 'Never mind,' I said.

'I had a thought,' I began, 'of taking up more lessons to do with my magic that is. Control it.'

Besr glanced at her, an eyebrow quirking. 'Lessons?' He leaned back on his throne. 'Sounds… nice. It is unneeded though. I will protect you.'

My gaze faltered. 'I wasn't thinking of the need, Besr. I was thinking of how fulfilling it might be.'

'Fulfilling?' Besr repeated with a scoff, already reaching for his hunting blade to polish it. 'I guess. But you could use that time for something useful—like meeting the ladies of the court.' He shrugged again, almost dismissively. 'But, if it makes you happy, I will provide it.'

I replied with a tight smile, my voice brittle as frost on a leaf. 'Thank you for your… help.'

Besr frowned, his tone laced with confusion. 'What? I'm being supportive! I said you should do it!'

I turned away, looking back toward the rain-slicked forest. my hands trembled slightly at her sides, my thoughts a swirling storm of frustration and doubt. 'Of course, dear,' I said quietly, my voice barely audible over the rising chorus of the rain.

The storm outside raged on, a reflection of the quiet discord between them. Besr remained seated, oblivious to the growing ache in my heart. And though we shared the same room, it felt as though miles of forest separated is, our worlds as distant as the storm clouds and the earth below.

* * *

I wished for sleep as the carriage rocked gently along the path home. Besr, with his many castles scattered across his kingdom, had one conveniently near our borders, only a few hours away.

The stars above shimmered in the velvet night, and I found myself wishing on each one as it flickered. I had dreamed that these visits would bring excitement, perhaps a sense of liberation. Instead, it seemed I had only traded one gilded prison for another.

I stifled a yawn, stretching my arms to shake the fatigue. Besr, seated across from me, watched with that soft, almost tender gaze of his.

'What?' I asked, arching an eyebrow at him.

'Nothing,' he replied with a lopsided smile.

I rolled my eyes, but a smirk tugged at my lips. I liked Besr well enough; his company was pleasant, even endearing at times. But Father's unyielding rules were a constant shadow. After sunset, we weren't allowed in the same room until our wedding day, as if mere proximity would unleash danger. And by daylight, Besr was always buried under the weight of his duties. I might as well have stayed in my chambers at home.

When we reached the castle, the familiar warmth of my sister's embrace awaited me.

'Aria!' Mel called, her face lighting up as she rushed forward.

'Mel!' I pulled her close, the comfort of her presence washing over me. 'It's so good to see you.'

'How was it?' she asked, her voice tinged with mischief. 'Tell me everything!'

'I would,' I said with a sigh, 'but Father expects us both at dinner.'

She scoffed, throwing her hands up. 'We could skip it, you know.'

'No, you cannot!' came Kal's sharp voice from the corridor, cutting through her scheming like a blade.

Mel groaned dramatically as if wounded by his rebuke. 'Fine,' she muttered, rolling her eyes. 'We'll go. But we should put on a show, sneak back here, and laugh about it later.'

I managed a weak smile, taking her hand and leading her to sit beside me on the edge of the bed. 'Mel, has Father mentioned anything about tonight?'

She shrugged nonchalantly. 'Not really. Why?'

'It's a diplomatic dinner,' I murmured, the words heavy on my tongue.

'So?' she asked, blinking at me.

I hesitated, then dropped the truth like a stone into a still pond. 'There will be kings, princes, nobles…'

Mel groaned again, this time flopping dramatically onto her back. 'They're here for my hand, aren't they?'

I nodded apologetically. 'I'm afraid so.'

'Perfect' she muttered, staring at the ceiling. 'Father never quits, does he?'

'Sorry.'

Her face broke into a mischievous grin. 'As long as none of them are named Dwayne, I think I'll survive.'

I laughed despite myself, the sound echoing softly in the room. Whatever the evening held, at least I wouldn't face it alone.

* * *

We waited for our father; the laughter and chatter of the room made my heart soar. I loved it when we could have dinner with the court, it was always so fun.

Fiddling with her heir's crown, Melody looked both regal and uneasy, a smaller version of my father's, a simple gold circle with the crescent moon and sun, symbolizing our family. Our family crest.

She looked beautiful in her red dress, with the gold detailed embroidery matching the simple golden chain and earrings she wore.

She painted her lips red and her hair was placed in a bun with her thorns twisting in and out of her hair. Only a couple strands of curls framed her face so beautifully.

Father sent his mistress to ready Melody for today; apparently, she was an opera singer, and therefore a devastatingly beautiful seductress.

Everyone said I took after my mother, but at that moment, as I looked at my sister I saw the portraits of my mother's youth in her.

I wore the golden tiara gifted to me by my mother; it was not the royal family's but from the Rose Court of the Fae kingdom. I was told it was my mother's favourite tiara at my age. My white dress was more simple than usual; the trip tired me too much to put any effort into getting ready. My hair was plaited together, with flowers randomly hidden within the gold strands

'Father,' we said in unison as my father arrived, his wife standing by him.

I always felt somewhat sorry for my stepmother; she was the Lady of the Court, held power and was known to be ruthless, but I knew her once upon a time before my father's cruelty took hold of her.

She arrived at court with hopes of great love. She was only twenty-five years our senior when she married him. I looked at her now; her blonde hair was once as free as the wind, flowing heavenly as she walked, the waves rippling. And now they were held captive in a high bun, her large crown the only accessory.

Her dress was heavy, layers and layers keeping her down filled with gold and jewels in the most beautiful designs. It looked almost painful as she breathed, walking as gracefully as if she was wearing a loose dress. The utter definition of a queen, not that my father ever noticed.

Sometimes when I looked at her I saw my future.

She took my hand in hers, 'Hello, darling.'

I squeezed her hand back, 'Your Majesty.' I curtsied nice and low before she nodded, bringing me back up.

She hugged me close, 'Oh, it has been too long since you have been at court; I have missed you.'

'Me too,' I whispered into her embrace until she let me go.

Melody hovered behind me, waiting to jump onto her.

Melody refused protocol, simply entrapping my stepmother in her arms, 'hi,' she whispered.

'Hello, Mel,'

'Come now girls,' my father shouted.

My stepmother rolled her eyes, Melody laughed while I bit my mouth to keep my hidden smile secret.

* * *

The great hall was beautiful, completely void of furniture except for the large table that stretched through the hall.

The stage was two thrones made from black stone and golden floral designs. These thrones were built by pure magic from our ancestors. But my father built the smaller thrones that sat a step behind the main thrones for us. Built from white stone, mine held designs of snow, whereas Melody's held roses.

We walked behind our parents, nodding to the nobles and ladies, most of whom never saw our faces. It was rare for us to attend court, especially an event with so many people. But Melody needed to take a new suitor, according to my father at least.

My father held my stepmother's hand in the air for all to see as she stepped up to the stage. She took her seat and he took his, their hands still falsely united, grinning to their adorning fans of simpering society.

Melody then took her seat, and finally, I sat down with a crooked smile. Let the show begin. Besr's smiling face shone out from the crowd and I knew at least this night we would spend together.

Twelve

Melody

❧

I watched the nobles and ladies of the court laughing beneath us, my cheek propped on my hand as I struggled to keep my eyes open.

'My love, why don't you go and dance?' my stepmother suggested gently.

'Dance?' I scoffed, shaking my head. 'I don't *dance*.'

She raised an eyebrow, her lips curving in a slight smile. 'That's a lie, and we both know it. Are you afraid you might *actually* enjoy the company of a noble befitting your station?'

I scowled at her. 'Not true.'

'Prove me wrong, then.'

With a sigh, I pushed myself up and began to make my way down the steps, feeling her satisfied gaze on my back.

When I found my father, he greeted me with a broad smile. 'My angel, you look beautiful as always,' he said, pressing a gentle kiss to my cheek.

'Thank you, Father.'

He nodded, his expression softening. 'I am proud of you, you know.'

I blinked, surprised. 'You are?'

'Of course. Thank you for following my rules.' He hesitated, his voice growing more sombre. "I know you hate the tower, but you understand it's necessary… because of the curse.'

I nodded, feeling the familiar weight of the word. *Curse.* 'I know, Father. But trust me—I would do anything to protect Aria.'

A shadow passed over his face. 'You could be taken too. Don't forget that.'

'I won't.'

He smiled again, and it felt like a rare gift, a small warmth blooming in my chest. 'Then will you grant your old father the honour of a dance?'

'Of course,' I said and allowed him to lead me onto the floor. The music softened, and we ignored the elaborate steps others performed around us, simply swaying together.

'Do you remember when I taught you how to dance?' He asked, his voice warm with nostalgia.

'How could I forget?' I smiled, glancing up at him. 'I ran from the dance teacher and demanded you teach me instead.'

He chuckled softly. 'And I played the song from your mother's and my wedding. You danced with all the joy she once did… even if your grace left something to be desired.' His eyes sparkled with a rare affection as he looked at me. 'But now look at you. Grace and elegance define you.'

I smiled, feeling the warmth in his words. 'Thank you, Father.'

'Let me tell you a secret,' he said, leaning in conspiratorially.

'Mhm?' I encouraged, curiosity piqued.

His voice dropped, a little unsteady but heartfelt. 'I'm glad you're not marrying him. If I lost you both at the same time, I think I might have broken.'

'Oh, Father…' I reached for his hand. 'Even when I marry, you will never lose me.'

His gaze searched mine, a quiet vulnerability in his question. 'Never?'

'Never,' I vowed, squeezing his hand.

He sighed, his shoulders relaxing just a little. 'I do want you to try, though. To find someone—someone true. It's the only—'

'The only way the curse will be lifted,' I finished for him.

'Just one person,' he pressed gently, the weight of his hope palpable.

I laughed lightly, the sound an odd mix of humour and resignation. 'You spent my whole life keeping me hidden, and now—'

'I kept you hidden from bad intentions,' he interrupted firmly. 'The men here are from families that bent the knee the day you were born. They are your loyal soldiers, protectors, and they come from good stock.'

'Fine,' I said, relenting with a sigh. 'Just one.'

'Please.'

'Okay, Father.'

His face softened into a smile, pride and relief radiating from him. 'That's my girl.'

* * *

I stayed in the shadows, tucked just out of view, watching the dancers move as if the world revolved around their perfectly timed steps. This was their realm—princes and nobles, ladies adorned in jewels, all spinning to the same predictable rhythm. It wasn't mine.

'Melody,' his voice, low and steady, reached me before he did.

I turned quickly, finding Kal standing behind me. His dark uniform, polished but plain, marked him as what he was: a guard. My guard, to be precise. But there was something about the way he carried himself—so composed, so confident—that he might as well have been a prince himself.

'What are you doing here?' I asked, my tone sharper than I intended.

'Ensuring your safety,' he said smoothly, the hint of a smile teasing at his lips. 'As always.'

I folded my arms, trying to steady my heart. 'Hardly necessary.

No one's going to attack me in a ballroom full of dignitaries.'

'Perhaps not.' He glanced at the dancers, his expression unreadable. 'But you seemed… stranded.'

'I'm perfectly fine,' I said, a little too quickly.

'Of course you are,' he replied, his voice softer now. He held out a hand, surprising me.

'I must dance with a man tonight.'

'Then find a man,' he said, his tone lightly amused.

'Fine. Dance with me.'

'Mel!'

'But just this once, would you indulge me?'

I stared at him, my breath catching.

'We shouldn't…'

'No one will notice,' I promised, barely above a whisper. 'My father gave me permission. Not in a room full of lords and ladies.'

It wasn't fair, the way he looked at me. Not pleading, not begging, just steady and patient.

'You know how this ends,' he murmured, more to himself than to me.

'Let me have this,' I said. 'Just for a moment. Before I am given to another person.'

Against my better judgment, I slipped my hand into his. His fingers were rough, calloused from years of wielding a sword, but they held mine gently as he led me onto the floor.

The music shifted into a waltz, slow and lilting. Kal moved with precision, his hand firm at my waist, guiding me effort-lessly into the steps. I followed, though my heart rebelled against every turn.

'You're a good dancer,' I said, my voice catching.

He smiled faintly. 'Not something a guard usually hears.'

'Well, if I remember correctly, you had a great teacher.'

He chuckled. 'She wasn't much of a teacher—more of a brat who refused to take no for an answer.'

I rolled my eyes. 'What happened to us?'

'We grew too old to be friends, Mel. You became a queen without me realising,' he said with a sad smile.

I wished to refuse his thoughts, to tell him we could be friends still, that there were no feelings between us, just for the mere hope of keeping him with me. Instead, I let the music carry us, spinning us into a world where rank and duty didn't matter.

But it wasn't real. It couldn't last.

'Melody,' he said quietly, his tone shifting. His hand tightened slightly at my waist, as though he was holding onto more than just the dance. 'You know this isn't—'

'I know,' I cut him off, my voice sharp with the ache I refused to show.

He hesitated, his jaw tightening. 'You deserve someone who can—'

'Stop,' I whispered, my steps faltering. 'Don't. Not tonight.'

For a moment, he said nothing. The music swelled around us, and the crowd blurred into golden light and shadows.

'You make it impossible,' he finally said, his voice so quiet I almost didn't hear it.

'Kal…' I began, but I couldn't finish.

The song ended too soon, and the spell broke. He stepped back, bowing slightly as the weight of the world returned to his shoulders. When he looked up, the warmth in his eyes was guarded, locked away behind duty and restraint.

'I'm sorry,' he said softly, and it sounded like he meant it.

'So am I,' I replied, my voice barely steady.

As he turned and melted back into the crowd, I was left

standing there, the ghost of his hand still lingering in mine. For a moment, I allowed myself to dream of a world where things could be different. But only for a moment.

* * *

'Why do you wish for me to get married?' I asked Aria after leaving the latest suitor she had thrown at me.

'It is the only way to get away from Father,' she said bluntly.

'That is not fair,' I replied, frustration bubbling to the surface. 'Why must I be married to be free? That's just wrong. My focus should be our people. I cannot stand the thought of a husband forcing his opinions down my throat—or worse, nursing a bruised ego.'

'What else are we meant to do?' Aria asked, sipping her drink from the golden flute she held.

'Do you hate this life so much? Father is good and kind and loves us.'

'Yes, but only when he can control us.' She turned to me, the coldness in her blue eyes replacing all the innocence and youth she once had. 'He loves us, yes, but he also refuses to let us live our lives. Both can be true. His worry keeps us living such a sheltered life—a life of doing nothing.'

'We are safe,' I countered.

'Is it worth living a life if it simply means being alive? That is not a life, Melody! Life is music and art and poetry and friendships and love! How can we even relate to poems and wonderful words when we have no memories or experiences of our own?'

'But you love him?' I asked her, quieter now.

'Yes, and I always will. But that doesn't mean I am content with the life he forces us to live.'

I nodded slowly. 'Once I am queen, we—'

'No, Mel,' she sighed, cutting me off. 'I refuse to wait any longer to live my life.'

'Aria,' I said, taking her hand in mine, 'we can do it. As long as we are together.'

She nodded, her grip firm. 'Always and forever.'

'Always and forever,' I agreed.

Thirteen

Aria

I ran through the gardens, my skirts whipping around my legs as if I could leave everything behind with each step. The cold air hit my face, sharp and biting, but I didn't care. Here, under the open sky, with the scent of roses swirling in the wind, I felt free—free in a way I was never allowed to be.

My guards followed at a distance, their watchful eyes tracking my every move. Only with them could I allow myself to ruin my clothes, to let my hair fall loose, to escape my title and simply *be*. The freedom of the gardens, of nature itself, was something so beautiful.

'Aria!'

The sharp, dark voice cut through the peace, freezing me in place. My father. At once, my guards straightened, their casual stances turning to formal bows and curtsies. Traitors.

Father's presence filled the garden, his towering figure blotting everything else. He was an intimidating man, with dark eyes and curls streaked with grey that only made him more handsome and powerful. Nothing about his features resembled mine.

'You look a mess,' he observed coldly, his gaze sweeping over me. He signalled to the guards. 'Take her to the tower.'

'What?' My voice wavered, but I held his gaze. 'But this is my only time to walk in the gardens,' I protested, my voice barely above a whisper, hoping the softness would soften him too.
  'I do not care.' His tone was dismissive, final. 'You are a princess, Aria. You have a reputation to uphold—a legacy to live up to. Your mother would never have let herself look so undignified.'

The words struck me like a blow, even though he tossed them at me with careless ease. *Your mother would never have let herself look so undignified.* My breath hitched, trying to hold back the tears that immediately began to build in the back of my throat.

'Father!' I protested as the guards closed in, taking hold of my arms. My shoulders slumped in defeat as they led me away. Over my shoulder, I saw him turn his back on me, walking away as if I were nothing more than an errant child.

* * *

'Aria, do not cry,' my stepmother soothed me. Her warmth only appeared to me and Mel, an old habit from her past self.

'I am not,' I lied as my throat burned, counting down from a hundred in my head in sevens, letting logic overrun the emotion.

'Come,' she said, patting the bed as she sat.

'You do not have to; the maids are drawing my bath.'

'It is okay; I will accompany you while we wait.'

'Thank you.' I took a seat in my bed, falling into my deep cushions, drawing my knees to my chest and crossing my arms across them. I groaned as I rested my head across my elbows.

'Aria, you must learn to speak your mind.'

'Like Mel? No, I am not her. And I do, just quietly; sometimes it is best; I cannot be brave like Mel. I am not her.'

'I know you could not be more different,' she chuckled, shaking her head slightly, 'but one skill on hers is that she is sly; she is smart and intelligent, but more than that, she is loud.'

'I have never been loud.'

'Just learn to pick your battles, okay?'

'Mhm,' words could no longer leave my lips, as I feared they would cause the tears to keep flowing.

'Would you like to study? It may give you an hour in the library?'

'No thank you; I think I will simply rest.'

'Okay,' she said, slapping her thighs as she stood up.

Fourteen

Melody

I waited until my stepmother walked down the steps before entering the room. Aria needed a moment to herself before I tried to cheer her up. She vanished into the bathroom, leaving me alone with my thoughts—and Kal.

I turned to my favourite guard, who stood against the wall, his brown hair falling gracefully around his face, the gold and black of his armour catching the light. He looked effortlessly beautiful, as always, so calm and composed.

'Hey,' I said, a playful note in my voice.

'Hello,' Kal replied bluntly, crossing his arms, as if the memories we shared meant nothing. His eyes followed me as I moved into the room.

'You're so much nicer to Aria than you are to me,' I teased, feigning a pout.

'Am not. Your stepmother is the one who helped her.'

'Are too. You don't play with me when I'm sad,' I complained, jutting my chin out.

'I didn't play with Aria either.'

'Promise?' I grinned, holding out my pinkie to him, but he just rolled his eyes and pushed my hand away. It was a small gesture, but dangerous enough. If anyone saw, he'd be in trouble—maybe worse than trouble.

'You're going to get me in trouble,' Kal muttered, glancing around nervously.

I smirked, stepping closer. 'Good.' Testing the boundaries. He quickly reassembled his stoic stance, his gaze steady and unyielding.

'Oh, are you giving me the silent treatment again?' I groaned dramatically. 'Tragic. Guess I'll just have to talk to myself. You know, when your only company is yourself and your sister, you start to realize how amazing you are.'

'Mel, stop bullying the guards,' came Aria's voice as she emerged from the bathroom, her freshly washed hair braided and gleaming, her golden silk gown draping elegantly around her.

'Then will you play with me?' I asked, brightening.

She smiled, illuminating the room with pure joy. 'What are we playing?'

'Roses vs. Snowflakes?'

Kal shuddered. 'No.'

'Oh, come on.' Aria pouted, crossing her arms.

'You're banned,' Kal reminded us with a pointed look. 'Do you not remember our childhood? Or when you turned sixteen? Or when you turned twenty?'

'So?' I shot back, raising an eyebrow.

'So Father said no, especially after last time,' Aria added, crossing her arms as if to imitate him.

'What's he going to do—ground us?' I spread my arms, gesturing around the opulent, confining tower where we'd been kept since the death of our mother. 'Oh wait…'

Aria chuckled and moved to the window, settling into her favourite spot on the ledge. 'I'm writing to Besr,' she announced, picking up a fresh piece of parchment.

I groaned. 'Fine, then I'll read.' I pulled another book from the shelf, feeling the weight of its well-worn pages. It's funny how I'd lived a thousand lives between these covers but never my own.

'Are you visiting him tomorrow?' I scribbled thoughts in the margins of my book, glancing up to watch Aria's response.

She nodded, dipping her pen into ink. Yes.

'Must be nice to have a fiancé Father cannot control,'

'You should use Dwayne to help you get what you want,' she replied, her lips falling into a small smile.

She chuckled softly, dipping her pen back into the ink with practised grace. The scratch of the nib against the parchment filled the silence between us, each stroke a soft reminder of the lives we lived within these walls. For a moment, I just watched her, catching the subtle curve of her smile as she crafted her response.

Everything I want is right here.

The smile slipped from my face as I glanced out the window at the sky beyond.

'Right here,' I repeated to myself, the annotations of my ideas sinking heavily onto the page.

Fifteen

Aria

The journey to the Fae kingdom was always bittersweet. It held a peculiar kind of magic—the kind that made time slow and nature breathe, where freedom lingered just beyond reach, cloaked in unseen chains. For me, it was a sanctuary where, for a few fleeting days, my name was not an extension of my father's power or my impending marriage. It was a place where, for a moment, I could pretend to be no one of consequence.

The carriage jolted over a root-strewn path, and I glanced at Melody, who sat across from me with her arms crossed, her gaze distant as she stared through the window. She looked like a painting that artists dream of capturing—an image of reluctant royalty, all fire and rebellion beneath her crown.

'Still not excited?' I teased, hoping to draw her out. Her eyes flicked to mine, then rolled away with a sigh.

'No,' she muttered, slumping further into her seat. 'The Fae kingdom may be beautiful, but it's a prison of rules. Even the trees feel like they're listening, just waiting to catch you in a lie.'

'You think everything is a prison,' I said softly. 'At least there, you'll be free of court duties. No suitors pestering you.'

She let out a dry laugh, hollow and edged with bitterness. 'Surrounded by guards, ours and theirs? I can't even breathe wrong without Aunt Talia snapping at me about proper decorum.'

I stayed silent, unable to argue with her. Aunt Talia had always been overly critical, though part of me wondered if it was her misguided way of protecting us. Melody, as the crown princess, was under a scrutiny that I could scarcely imagine.

But Aunt Talia's sharp gaze always lingered longer on me, dissecting my every flaw. She favoured Melody—perhaps because I reminded her of a ghost of my mother. Would I be able to look at the clone of Melody's if she died? The pain would be too heartbreaking. Or perhaps I was simply too much like my father: too willing to bend to the court's demands, too eager to play the dutiful daughter.

'She only wants the best for you,' I murmured. 'Aunt Talia taught you to control your magic when no one else would.'

'Yes, but at what cost?' Melody's fingers traced the rose-inked patterns on her shoulders, a habit she returned to when we visited the Fae. 'Every time we visit, it's like stepping back into a role I never wanted. I have to be… you.'

I blinked. 'What do you mean, me?'

'A good princess,' she said the words as a joke, but something tasted like envy. 'I have to watch my language, my clothes, even how I breathe. Everything is judged. And you—you're perfect at it. You handle father's moods, the court politics, the nobles. You're everything they want me to be.'

Her words stung more than I cared to admit. Did she think

I wanted this life of constant performance? Did she think I enjoyed placating our father's volatile temper and navigating the endless labyrinth of court intrigue? In her eyes, perhaps I was the obedient daughter, a gleaming reflection of what a princess should be. But only because the rebel had already been taken.

Sixteen

Melody

I woke with a start as the carriage jolted to a sudden halt, sleep tearing away from my eyes. Kal's face appeared at the door, his expression taut and focused. The subtle raise of his perfectly arched brows, the way his eyes scanned the shadows—those tells only meant one thing.

'What?' I asked, trying to shake off the remnants of sleep. Aria was already pressing her face to the window, searching for some hint of adventure beyond the glass.

Leaning forward, I repeated, 'Kal, what is it?'

'Bandits,' he murmured, his voice low and urgent.

'Bandits?' I turned to peer out the window, my heart plummeting as I caught sight of our guards, their bodies pierced with arrows. These weren't bandits—they were soldiers, cruel and efficient.

The muffled sounds of steel clashing filled the air, punctuated by screams of pain. Outside, our soldiers were locked in battle, their cries cutting through the stillness of the forest.

'Protect the princesses!' Kal shouted, his sword flashing from its scabbard in a swift, practised motion.

'Protect Aria!' I ordered, reaching under my skirt to draw the blade I kept strapped to my thigh. The layers of silver lace and black floral embroidery that the Fae insisted upon now felt like a trap. The dress was a masterpiece of fantasy, but in this moment, it was a hindrance.

A soldier's scream rang out, loud and guttural, just beyond the carriage. My pulse quickened as I heard the sickening crunch of bone, followed by another pained cry.

'Mel!' Aria cried, her voice trembling with fear.

'I love you,' I whispered, conjuring a barrier of thorns around her. Blood-red roses bloomed viciously among the spikes, their sharp edges glistening in the faint light.

'Melody!' she screamed, pressing her hands against the carriage door.

'Do not touch the thorns!' I warned, but she ignored me.

'Melody, don't leave this fucking carriage!' Aria shouted, but I was already outside, my boots sinking into the mud as I landed beside Kal.

'Where are you going?' he asked, his eyes wide.

'The carriage stopped,' I replied, wiping mud from my dress. 'The driver—'

'Is likely dead,' he finished for me, glancing toward the front of the carriage where another scream erupted. 'I need to get you out of here.'

'No,' I insisted, grabbing his arm. 'Get Aria to safety!'

Kal's eyes softened, but his jaw was set. 'Mel, you're the crown princess. It's you I need to protect.'

'But...'

'What?' he pressed, urgency lacing his voice.

I smiled, a pang of sadness piercing through the chaos. 'This is the longest conversation we've had since we were kids. I want more… scattered through our future. Don't you dare die on me.'

His lips quirked into a sad smile. 'I'll try. But whatever happens—stay safe. And, please, stop being so damn stubborn. You stay in that carriage.'

'I'm never stubborn,' I shot back with a faint grin, sitting back down inside.

He chuckled softly. 'Until we meet again.' And with that, he was gone, leaping into the driver's seat and cracking the reins.

Inside, Aria's eyes locked onto mine, her lips trembling as another scream tore through the air outside.

'What?' I snapped.

Raising her hands, she transformed the thorns into ice, their petals shimmering with frost. 'Never do that again,' she hissed.

I gasped. Aria had never used her Fatal power before. She barely used her magic at all and had refused to learn proper spells.

'I can't see our guards.'

'Nasir?' I asked, searching the chaos outside.

She shook her head, her voice wavering. 'He's gone. What's happening?'

'I don't know, darling.' I stroked her hair, trying to soothe her as the screams outside grew fainter. 'We just need to reach Aunt Talia.'

Suddenly, the carriage lurched forward again, the sudden speed throwing me against the seat. The sound of hooves pounding against the dirt replaced the screams, but my heart still thundered in my chest.

'Kal?' I called out. 'What's happening?'

'We're barely near the border,,' Kal replied, his voice strained. 'But this isn't close to the Rose Court. It's close to the Dark Fae kingdom.'

Aria's eyes went wide. 'But we're royals. They can't touch us!'

Kal gave a bitter laugh. 'The nobles can't, no. But if bandits kill us on the road, who's to blame?'

'I should step out,' Aria offered, gripping the dagger she'd pulled from her pearl-studded purse.

'That tiny thing?' I scoffed. The dagger was more ornament than weapon, wrapped in delicate silver chains.

'Hey, it can still be deadly,' she shot back, tying on her gold-trimmed cape and pulling the hood over her hair.

'Only if you know how to use it.'

'I do,' she huffed, but her bravado wavered.

I jumped down from the carriage, extending my hand to help her down. As her feet touched the ground, I scanned the area. 'Kal?' I called again, but there was no answer.

'He was just here,' Aria whispered, panic creeping into her voice. 'Where did he go?'

My stomach clenched. 'I… I don't know.' I rounded to the front of the carriage, but the driver's seat was empty. A soft flicker of gold caught my eye—a piece of Kal's scarf, damp with rain and tinged with the scent of honey he always wore. I clutched it, feeling a hollow ache as I realized what it meant.

'Melody!' Aria's panicked scream jolted me back. I turned to see her trembling, eyes darting around the dark forest that now surrounded us. The air was filled with the haunting echoes of laughter and the thundering approach of horses.

'What the hell are we going to do?' I whispered to myself, my mind racing as Aria's breaths came faster and faster. I closed

my eyes, trying to gather my thoughts.
I couldn't afford to panic. Not now.
For Aria's sake, I had to be strong.

Seventeen

Aria

'Damn it, Mel,' I muttered, my voice cracking as I caught my breath. The forest around us was dense, darkening as the sun dipped beneath the horizon. Shadows played across Melody's face, softening her fierce gaze as she pulled me close, her fingers trailing over the scars that hadn't been there before—each one a story I hadn't yet shared.

'What? Aria, are you okay?' she whispered, her voice full of worry. Her hand lingered on a jagged scar by my collarbone, her thumb tracing it lightly as if to take the pain for herself.

'Yeah,' I breathed, nodding, my voice barely steady.

'Then follow my lead,' she said, her tone firm but familiar. Without hesitation, she tugged at the ornate cape draped over my dress, her fingers nimble, practised from years of tending to me—whether braiding my hair in the morning or fixing the messes I constantly got myself into.

'Follow your lead?' I echoed, matching her movements almost

instinctively. We had always been in sync, two halves of the same soul, each one knowing the other's next move. I mimicked her as she slipped out of the heavy layers, peeling away our roles as princesses, leaving us exposed but lighter.

She paused, looking over her shoulder as if she could sense eyes in the shadows. 'It seems the ones tracking us, killing everyone in their way, are—'

'What?' My patience wavered as I waited for her to finish, nerves fraying. Her eyes flickered, barely able to meet mine.

'Kal said they're bandits,' she whispered, her voice barely audible, almost as if she were afraid the very word would summon them.

'Bandits?' I whisper-shouted, the disbelief thick in my voice.

She nodded, a small, tired smile pulling at her lips. 'Yes, bandits.' She threw her tiara of jewels back into the carriage without a thought.

A laugh, bitter and short, escaped me. 'What are we going to do?'

'Hide your weapon,' she replied without missing a beat, her hand hovering over mine, her warmth a steadying anchor.

'What?' I asked, my voice faltering, while she used her dagger to slice through the laces of my dress.

'And get rid of the gowns.' She didn't wait for a response, instead moving behind me to untie the laces at my back, careful but quick. Her touch was gentle, as if she were holding fragile glass. She knew the weight of our station had always sat heavier on me, and now, more than ever, I could feel it lifting as she shed the last layer, leaving me in a simple white silk shift.

'Why?'

'Just listen to me, okay?' She looked at me, and for a moment, I saw the worry she tried to mask behind her usual confidence.

This was Melody—the one who had always shielded me, the one who stayed by my side through every scraped knee and whispered secret.

'Alright,' I whispered, trying to match her steadiness.

'Lose this layer and the cape.' She bundled the discarded clothes and, with a practised flick of her wrist, created a patch of roses that sprang from the earth—soft petals and thorns woven into a bush that concealed our garments. Her magic was gentle and purposeful, just like her.

My fingers curled around the necklace I wore. Melody's hand covered mine, her eyes pleading.

'Please, no.'

Her grip tightened, the warmth of her palm grounding me. 'It's obvious, Aria.'

'Bandits won't know a royal sigil when they see one.'

I nodded, surrendering.

'Fine, but if anyone asks, it's an engagement present from some duke or lord—not a king.'

'Good,' I said, satisfaction.

She reached up, adjusting my hair, taking the white ribbon I always kept on my wrist and securing it back, her movements as practised as if she had done it a thousand times. 'Now we look like ladies-in-waiting—still elegant and graceful, but not important enough to be taken hostage or hurt.'

'How do you know all this?' I whispered, a smirk edging its way onto my lips.

A smirk of her own mirrored mine. 'It's what the main character would do.'

I rolled my eyes. 'We're not in a romance novel.'

'Well, I just hope it's not a bloody tragedy,' she remarked, her voice light but laced with a hint of fear.

I scoffed, adjusting the thin ribbon. I could feel her watching me, her gaze heavy with worry she'd never voice. 'You think this will really work?'

Her hand brushed my shoulder. 'We'll make it work. Together. Well, and the gifts blessed on us. We have charm and luck on our side.'

I nodded, steeling myself. Whatever lay ahead, we would face it as we always had—side by side.

Eighteen

Melody

I widened my eyes, letting them grow soft and round, my lips trembling slightly—a practised look, one that always seemed to pull others under its spell. The man in black dismounted his horse with smooth, purposeful movements. Within seconds, he was at my side, reaching for my hand.

His skin was a shade of light brown, lighter than mine, and his eyes a gentle green—not the vibrant green of a forest, but something softer, pale and calming, like new moss. Yet there was an intensity in his gaze that made it impossible to discern his true intentions or lineage.

'What is your name?' he asked, his voice smooth and deceptively warm.

'Mine?' I replied, my voice as delicate as I could make it, barely more than a whisper.

'Yes.'

'Rose,' I answered, keeping my voice steady despite the slight tremor in my fingers.

His fingers cruelly traced the ink across my collarbone. 'Rose?' he echoed, a faint smile tugging at his lips. With practised gallantry, he unfastened his thick black cloak and draped it over my shoulders, as though he were my savoir. The weight of it settled over me, hiding the involuntary shivers that raced down my arms.

'What is a beauty like you doing in the mud, my dear red rose?' His voice was rich, dripping with feigned concern.

'The guards,' I began, letting my gaze drop in an act of shame, 'they stayed behind to protect the princesses. We were abandoned.'

He sighed with what appeared to be genuine regret, though his eyes betrayed him—they were devoid of softness or care. His thumb brushed my cheek, and I fought back the urge to recoil, forcing my expression to remain innocent and fragile.

'They do not care about the Fae,' he said with mock sympathy. 'Oh, I am sorry, my dear. If I had known a Fae rose as beautiful as you were hidden in those carriages, I never would have ordered my men to attack.' His words sounded sincere, but the gleam in his eye told another story. His thumb lingered, stroking my cheek with a silent taunt.

'Your men?' I asked, though I already knew the answer.

'Yes,' he replied, not a hint of guilt in his tone. 'As an apology, perhaps you'd come back with me?'

I hesitated, drawing in a steadying breath. 'And my sister?'

'Your sister?' His eyes flickered briefly, assessing.

'Yes. Her name is Snow,' I said, keeping my tone light and compliant, as he seemed to want.

'Snow?' he repeated, his eyebrows lifting in mild surprise.

'She's named for her white and gold hair,' I explained, forcing a shy smile.

'Very well,' he agreed with a nod. 'You'll ride with me.'

'And my sister?'

'She'll ride with my men.'

I hesitated, casting a quick, worried look toward Aria, my sister, who stood as fierce as any blade.

Her chin was raised, shoulders squared, defiance blazing in her eyes. 'I'll be fine, sister,' she said, her voice strong, steady, and unshaken.

Reluctantly, I nodded, my stomach twisting as the man's arm found its way around my waist, pulling me close with an unsettling familiarity. He led me forward, his hand drifting to my lower back, firm and possessive.

'Come,' he said, his voice laced with satisfaction.

Suppressing the flicker of anger and disgust threatening to break my composure, I nodded, swallowing down the emotions and slipping into the role I'd chosen. His hand remained at my back, guiding me toward an uncertain fate.

Nineteen

Aria

❦

I found myself sitting between two men, each with a single flame tattoo etched into their forearms. We were outside, though I couldn't quite place where. It wasn't a garden, nor a clearing—it was just… somewhere. The dark sky stretched endlessly above, and the only light came from the flickering campfire at the centre of the circle. The men roared with laughter, their voices thick with drink.

'Where is my sister?' I asked the man beside me, forcing calm into my voice.

'The boss wanted some time alone with her,' he replied casually. He was younger than the rest, lanky, with eyes that seemed too wide for his gaunt face.

'Alone?' My voice trembled despite my best efforts to keep steady.

'Look,' the man on my right, a burly figure with cruel, coal-black eyes, cut in. 'You and your sister are lucky your faces are sweet. If it wasn't for that, he would've driven a sword through both your hearts without a second thought.'

I swallowed hard, casting furtive glances at the men around the fire. Some had the pointed ears of the Fae, others bore the rebel tattoos of the Outlands, and a few were unmarked—men with no hint of their origins. I couldn't decide which were more dangerous.

Nodding slowly, I sent a silent gratitude to whatever force had blessed us with beauty and charm—a small mercy in a world as cruel as this. 'May I take my leave?' I asked, hoping they would let me go without incident.

The burly man beside me seized my wrist. 'Sweetheart,' he murmured, his grip tightening, 'the boss said hands off your sister, but you? You could belong to one of us.'

'Belong?' I echoed, my stomach twisting. 'What do you mean?'

'It's better to be protected by one than used by all,' he said, leaning in close, the reek of ale on his breath.

Before I could respond, another man stepped in. He was older, with greying hair and rough stubble. He pulled my hand free from the brute's grasp. 'Shut your trap,' he barked. 'What? Am I the only one who doesn't want to drag an angel down to hell?' He cackled a harsh sound that grated on my nerves. 'Some men like their demons, after all.'

'Enough,' the younger man from earlier interjected, his voice low and firm. 'We look after our women here.' He took my arm and guided me back to the log beside him.

I turned to him, my voice a mere whisper. 'What do they mean?'

'Do not worry, angel,' he said, his expression softening. 'Just smile, pour the wine, and I'll make sure no one touches you.

You'll stay with the other girls.'

My breath hitched in my throat. Was that truly the better alternative? To play the part, to be nothing more than a pretty face? I nodded, the weight of my fear pinning me down, and got to my feet.

I wasn't alone in serving the men. A handful of other girls flitted around the fire, draped in silk and chiffon, their smiles unnaturally bright. I watched them, trying to understand how they kept their spirits so seemingly high. To my surprise, the men around us weren't lecherous. They accepted their wine with nods and half-smiles, refraining from the crude comments or leering glances I had braced myself for.

But even as I moved among them, pouring wine with a forced smile, I couldn't shake the chill that crept into my bones.

Was this respite from their cruelty just a trick, a momentary illusion? And how long could I keep pretending everything was fine before it all came crashing down?

Twenty

Melody

He opened the door to a bleak room. It wasn't filthy, just dull and lifeless. In the centre was a single, large bed, a small wardrobe pressed against the wall, and no window to speak of. The air felt heavy, like it hadn't been touched by daylight in years.

'Please,' I pleaded, my voice quivering. 'My sister and I are just helpers. The princesses don't even know our names.'

A slow smile crept onto his lips, his eyes gleaming with amusement. 'You're more sly than I gave you credit for.'

'Excuse me?' I feigned confusion, though my heart pounded in my chest.

'Don't get me wrong,' he drawled, leaning against the door frame. 'It was entertaining, being manipulated by those big brown eyes of yours. But I knew exactly what you were doing. I simply didn't care. You played your role well, and I want you to continue. I do not care who you were.'

I took a step back, keeping my gaze steady. 'Please, I beg you… just keep A—Snow safe.'

'Oh, she will be,' he assured me, his tone turning almost syrupy. 'She'll be treated as if she were my late lover's sister… practically royalty.'

I blinked. 'Excuse me?'

'My last lover,' he said casually, adjusting the tie of his robe. 'She passed.'

'How?' I asked, my eyes narrowing.

'Quite naturally,' he answered, a smirk curling his lips.

'Funny,' I said, crossing my arms as the mask I'd worn began to slip. 'I find that hard to believe.'

He shrugged, unconcerned, and for a moment, I saw him for what he truly was—a predator draped in silken robes, as pretty as his heart was cold. There was no kindness behind those eyes; only the cold, calculating sharpness of a transaction.

'So,' he continued, studying me with an unsettling intensity, 'what do you say? I need a new woman to keep the house running, and you need protection. Look after the women here, and in return, you'll have nearly as much power over those men as I do. Not quite as much, but enough.' He tilted his head, his eyes glittering. 'You wanted to play the game, so you may as well win it. Be my queen.'

I swallowed hard, the taste of my own desperation bitter on my tongue. 'Fine,' I said through clenched teeth. 'But get her out of that room.'

He grinned. 'Gladly, once our deal is sealed. You both may rest tonight, but tomorrow… I expect grins and laughter from the two of you.'

* * *

'Snow!' I whispered as I embraced her tightly, her small frame trembling against mine.

'Is that our new name?' she murmured into my ear.

'It always was our second name,' I whispered back. 'Might as well put it to use.'

I pulled back, tilting her chin up to examine her face. 'Are you feeling okay?' I asked, pressing the back of my hand to her forehead.

'Yes, but… what are we going to do?'

'Listen,' I said, lowering my voice. 'These men… they're powerless. There's no Fae blood in them—at least, none strong enough to bind us.'

'They're not noble?'

'No. They can lie, which means they lack the magic that would make them truly dangerous to us. They're just… pretty.'

'Like us,' she said with a small, rueful smile.

I nodded. 'I thank the Ancestors for our beauty every day. It's a weapon they underestimate.'

Her eyes searched mine. 'I have a plan,' I whispered, stroking her hair.

'Please, no killing,' she pleaded, her voice barely above a whisper.

'Not yet,' I promised, though the edge in my tone made her frown. She didn't like that answer, but she nodded all the same, a small crease of worry forming between her brows.

'I will get us home,' I assured her, brushing away the tears gathering in her eyes with my thumb. 'I promise.'

Her lips trembled, but she nodded again, leaning into my touch. 'I know,' she whispered. 'I trust you.'

And as we clung to each other in that cold, lifeless room, surrounded by enemies lurking in every shadow, I made a silent vow: I would see us both free. No matter what it took.

Twenty-One

Aria

⚬⚬⚬

'Smile, Aria,' Melody whispered urgently, her fingers deftly smoothing the fabric of my dress. I looked down at myself, turning slowly to take in the flowing yellow dress. It was much lighter than anything I had ever worn—simple layers that swirled with each movement. The material felt foreign against my skin, more rough than I was used to.

'What are these clothes?' I murmured, fidgeting with the hem.

'They're clean, and that's all we need,' Melody replied as she twisted my hair into a loose bun, letting strands cascade freely over my shoulders. 'Now listen: don't flirt, but be friendly. Serve, but stand your ground. Understand?'

I nodded, taking a deep breath. 'Thanks, Mel.'

'Rose,' she corrected me in a hushed tone.

'Rose,' I repeated softly, adjusting to the name we were forced to adopt.

She glanced around the room before lowering her voice further. 'It won't be long. How would you feel about… using your ice?'

I tilted my head, giving her a sharp look. My irritation was clear in my eyes.

'Right, no killing,' she muttered, setting the brush down on a side table. 'I just need us to be in the same place. We'll leave tonight.'

'Tonight?' I asked, trying to mask my shock.

'Yes,' she affirmed, her tone resolute. 'I just need my hand in yours so I don't worry about you. Today, I'll find the exit to this place.'

I nodded slowly. Melody's confidence was the anchor I needed, but beneath my outward calm, fear gnawed at me.

'Now,' she whispered with a faint smile, 'smile and laugh like everything is fine.']

* * *

A woman stepped into the room, perhaps only a year or two older than me, dressed in layers of light pink silk that whispered against the floor as she walked. A delicate golden chain rested on her forehead, giving her the air of someone important. Her presence was calm, almost disarming, though I couldn't decide if it was genuine or calculated.

'You've been requested by a highly esteemed guest,' she announced, her voice light and almost teasing.

I nodded politely, studying her. 'Who are you?'

'Jas,' she replied smoothly, a hint of a smirk playing on her lips. 'I'm Jafar's sister, he is the King of Thieves. I run the women of the house.'

'Are you… bandits?' I asked, keeping my voice low.

'Not exactly,' she said, amusement flashing in her eyes. 'We're an army for hire.'

'So, someone hired you to kill… us?'

'Not you,' she corrected with a sharpness that cut through her earlier levity. 'The princesses.'

I swallowed hard, my heart thudding in my chest. 'And what about you? What are you?'

'Me?' She let out a soft laugh, tilting her head as though the question amused her. 'I'm just a woman trying to survive in this world.'

'Are you Fae?'

'Yes, half,' she answered, her tone more clipped now. 'This is an army of hybrids and outcasts. You'll get used to how we do things here.' Leaning closer, she added in a conspiratorial whisper, 'Between us, he's your best chance of staying alive.'

'Thanks… I guess,' I muttered, her words settling uneasily in my chest.

Jas straightened, her pink silks rustling softly. Her smirk

returned, and for a moment, I thought I saw something genuine in her expression—compassion, perhaps, or pity. But it was gone as quickly as it appeared, replaced with the cool detachment of someone who had mastered the art of survival.

* * *

Taking a deep breath, I stepped into the dimly lit room, a jug of wine in my hands. I tried to project the confidence Melody had drilled into me, letting my movements appear fluid, and graceful. The room seemed empty at first glance, its silence pressing. I placed the jug on the table, the long yellow skirt of my dress swirling softly as I turned.

The quiet shattered with a sudden crash behind me.

I spun around, my heart hammering. A towering figure emerged from the shadows, his presence commanding and unrelenting, like a storm rolling in. His dark clothing blended seamlessly with the dim light, but his wild, curly hair seemed to defy the gloom, a chaotic crown. Striking green eyes gleamed as they slowly moved up my body, their intensity sending a shiver down my spine.

'Who—' I began, but he cut me off with a sharp, 'Hush.'

He strode forward, each step purposeful, almost predatory. The closer he got, the more the air seemed to thin, his presence filling every corner of the room.

'I—no, I will not hush! How dare you even—'

Before I could finish, he grabbed me by the waist and hauled me up as though I weighed nothing. A gasp escaped my lips as I found myself slung over his shoulder, his touch hot against my skin. My pulse quickened—a wild mix of fear and something else I didn't want to name.

'Excuse me!' I yelled, pounding my fists against his back. 'I am engaged! You can't just touch me like this! Do you even know—'

He slammed me against the wall, pinning my wrists above my head with one hand. The cool stone bit into my back, and his eyes bored into mine, blazing with a dangerous intensity. His breath was warm against my face, and his voice, low and sharp as a blade, cut through the tension.

'Do you want to die?'

'No,' I whispered, the fight draining from me as his words hung heavy in the air.

'Then quiet,' he commanded, releasing my wrists with an almost dismissive flick of his fingers as if I were nothing more than a nuisance.

I scowled, crossing my arms like a petulant child, frustration boiling beneath the surface. 'Fine,' I muttered, cheeks flushed with anger and humiliation.

He chuckled softly, the sound low and taunting, sending chills racing down my spine. 'Good,' he said, his gaze lingering on me for a moment longer, his eyes alight with something I couldn't place. Then he turned away, his movements as fluid as they were commanding.

For a moment, I stood there, breathless and shaken, brushing off my yellow dress in an attempt to recover my composure. But before I could gather my thoughts, his hand shot out, grabbing me again.

'What now?' I managed, my voice sharp with indignation.

He didn't answer. Instead, he hoisted me effortlessly, his grip unrelenting, and began running through the winding corridors of the derelict cave. The walls blurred past in the dim light, the sound of his boots striking the stone echoing in my ears.

Panic and fury swirled within me, but I bit my tongue, saving my words for when I'd have the chance to use them wisely. Wherever he was taking me, I'd need to be ready.

Twenty-Two

Melody

'Rose, my sweet,' Jafar called, his voice smooth with authority, 'greet my dear friend with wine.'

The men sat on the floor, surrounded by cushions of silk and velvet. In the centre, a low wooden table held only two golden cups, each delicate as a whisper.

'This is your newest lover?' The stranger stood, his gaze narrowing as it roved over me. His eyes never wavered, carrying a quiet intensity that almost made me blush. Confidence poured off him like a heatwave, compelling and unyielding. But just as quickly, he seemed to tire of me, turning back to his business, leaving me to serve.

'Is she not beautiful?' Jafar boasted, leaning back with a triumphant grin. 'I picked her out of the mud.'

'The mud?' the stranger echoed with a faint sneer as he

lowered himself back onto the cushions. His elbow propped him up while he sipped from his tiny golden cup, eyes darkening with something inscrutable. 'I don't see the task completed.'

A thrill of recognition shot through me. *This was the man behind the slaughter of those I loved. The man whose orders brought death to my doorstep.* He was striking, but not in any way that mattered—brown eyes, black hair, patterns of ink trailing down his arms. His eyes were rimmed with kohl, his ears pointed sharply, marking him as Fae.

But still—nothing special. Nothing that a quick, precise strike couldn't remedy.

'Whatever do you mean?' Jafar asked, his voice slipping into that dangerous tone reserved for men like him.

The stranger's smile was a razor's edge. 'Where are the girls I requested?' His politeness evaporated as he rose once more, his presence expanding until it filled the room.

'I—'

There it was. Confirmation. My grip tightened on the jug of wine. It would be so easy—one flick of my wrist, one deadly strike. But Aria, my sister, was still ensnared, her powers contained, her fate tangled in this game. For now, I would remain a ghost in their midst—seen, yet invisible.

'They are Fae royalty,' the stranger said, his voice low and measured. 'Descendants of the third bloodline—neither Light nor Dark. Their mother's family is archaic, ancient even among us. I asked for them untouched. Disappointment will be... costly, if they are harmed.' His hands slammed onto the table, each word a sharpened blade aimed at Jafar.

'Then why take them at all?' Jafar asked, feigning confusion.

A smile ghosted over the stranger's lips. 'Spoils of war,' he said, stepping back, his tone almost playful. 'I respect their lineage, but I do not care for them as people. I wish only to see their powers—two mighty bloodlines mingled. If the prophecy is true, one could be the most powerful creature to walk this world. Imagine a shadow beast… a living nightmare.'

'We couldn't capture them,' Jafar admitted reluctantly. 'But they are isolated—vulnerable.'

The stranger hummed thoughtfully, pacing with hands clasped behind his back. 'So you failed.'

'Rose, come here.' Jafar's voice broke the tension, his eyes flicking toward me as he stood.

'Yes?' I approached, keeping my expression serene.

The stranger's gaze was sharp as he studied me. 'Mistress? Or pawn?' His voice caressed the air like silk, but his eyes were relentless.

'A lady-in-waiting,' Jafar snapped. 'To serve the princess.'

The stranger ignored him, taking my hand and running his thumb along my palm. A shiver traced up my spine as he examined it with eerie precision. 'Soft hands for someone who serves royalty,' he murmured. 'Unblemished, unscarred.'

I held my head high. 'The harder tasks are left to the servants.'

He smiled, a slow, knowing curve of his lips. 'Curious. I had heard the king was mad, allowing only seasoned guards near his daughter. And certainly not… young ladies like you.'

Jafar's temper flared, his voice booming, 'What are you insinuating? Enough of your games!'

But the stranger merely looked bored, as if Jafar were no more than an irritating fly. In a fluid motion, he pulled me into his embrace, so quickly I dropped the jug, spilling wine across the floor. Crimson spread across the silken rugs, staining the hem of my white gown.

'Unhand her!' Jafar roared, grabbing my wrist and yanking

me back. The stranger's grip loosened almost lazily, as if I had simply slipped through his fingers. Yet the nod he gave me sent a strange calm through my veins.

'No,' Jafar hissed, his face inches from mine. 'She owes me. My men screamed for her sister, and I protected them. She belongs to me.'

My eyes rolled, and with a subtle flick of my finger, I called forth the thorns. They pierced him like needles threading through cloth, twisting deeper with every breath he took.

'Quite unfortunate,' I said, my tone almost regretful as he gasped. 'He was charming, in a foolish sort of way.'

'Shit,' he muttered, collapsing to the ground as blood spilt across the grey silk beneath him.

The stranger watched with mild interest, a flicker of amusement in his dark eyes.

I turned toward him, a smile playing on my lips. 'Scared?'

He stepped closer, one arm slipping around my waist, his touch firm but not unkind. 'No,' he said, his voice like velvet. 'But you have my attention.'

Before I could respond, darkness erupted from him, wrapping around me like a shroud. My legs gave way, but his arms held me steady.

'I'm not rising to it, love,' he whispered, his breath hot against my ear. 'Not yet.'

And in that moment, I realized that this game had only just begun.

Aria

The handsome stranger placed me into the black carriage. *Placed* would be too gentle a word. *Thrown* would be more fitting.

'I will destroy this entire carriage!' I screamed, thrashing against the soft purple cushions, my fists pounding against the velvet walls. The air crackled with the faintest hint of magic, my anger threatening to spill over.

He leaned casually against the carriage door, his smirk a mocking slash on his face. 'Be my guest,' he said with a lazy drawl. 'Feel free to return to those savages. Is that what you'd like, princess?'

His hood slipped back, revealing sharp, pointed ears that glinted in the dim light.

'You're Fae?' I demanded, my voice dropping to a whisper.

'Yes,' he replied simply, meeting my gaze without hesitation.

'Do you know my grandparents?'

He gave a half-shrug. 'Not personally, but I know of them, of course.'

'I still don't trust you.'

He smiled faintly, his eyes darkening. 'That's smart.'

I bit my lip, forcing myself to hold his gaze. 'Where is my sister?'

'She's coming,' he assured me.

A tense silence followed, broken only by the rhythmic clatter of the carriage wheels. The weight of unspoken fears pressed heavily against me. Finally, I softened. 'Fine. But… did you save anyone else? Did anyone survive?'

I dared to hope, my heart fluttering with fragile possibility.

'No.'

His words hit me like a blow. My breath caught, and I dropped my gaze to my hands, watching as tiny, delicate snowflakes swirled around my fingertips, drifting away like fragments of a broken dream.

'I'm… sorry.'

I nodded, swallowing hard, the weight of the loss almost crushing me. He reached out, his fingers unexpectedly gentle as they closed around mine.

'But you can't use your powers, understand?' His voice was soft, yet it held an edge of command.

'I—I can't control them when I'm… upset.'

He nodded slowly, his grip tightening slightly. 'Then let me help you rest.'

I tilted my head, narrowing my eyes at him. 'I don't trust you to do that.'

'I cannot lie,' he murmured, his voice low and steady. 'I promise you, you will simply wake up refreshed.'

I hesitated, my mind warring with itself. But exhaustion

won. 'Fine,' I whispered, and the world went dark as my body succumbed to his magic.

* * *

When I awoke, I found myself leaning against someone's shoulder. Blinking away the haze of sleep, I realized it was the lady of the house. Her presence was both warm and commanding, her gown a cascade of pale gold and cream that glimmered faintly in the dim carriage light.

'Hello, sweet girl,' she greeted, her voice like the first hint of dawn after a long night.

I glanced around, disoriented, my gaze darting to the stranger who stood near the carriage door. Then back to the lady. 'What happened?'

Her eyes softened as she looked down at me. 'I saved my girls. Now rest. I fear it will be a long journey.'

'My sister?'

She squeezed my hand, her touch firm and grounding. 'Safe,' she confirmed, her eyes holding a strength that made me believe her instantly.

I let out a breath I didn't know I was holding, relief washing over me. Perhaps it was foolish to trust her so easily, but something in her gaze was undeniably reassuring.

I closed my eyes again, allowing the lull of the road and her steady presence to draw me back into the depths of sleep.

Twenty-Four

Melody

'**D**id you find anyone else?' I asked, my voice barely above a whisper, the words scraping my throat like shards of glass.

'No.'

The carriage continued its steady rumble beneath me, the sound a dull ache in my bones. I stared down at my trembling hands. 'So… all my friends are dead?' The words cracked, barely making it past my lips.

I forced myself to focus, counting backwards from one hundred in sevens, clinging to the cold comfort of logic to keep the tears at bay.

'They were your servants,' he said, his voice low, almost indifferent.

'They were our only company for our entire lives!' I screamed, the anguish tearing out of me.

He tilted his head, studying me with an expression I couldn't decipher. 'I've never seen a princess mourn a servant before.'

'Perhaps because princesses aren't meant to mourn,' I shot back, my voice shaking. 'But...' I met his gaze, unflinching. 'Who's here to tell me to stop?'

He held my stare for a moment longer, then reached into his cloak and pulled out a shimmering piece of fabric. 'Here.' He handed me the gold scarf. 'We found this among the wreckage.'

My breath caught in my chest. I recognized it immediately—the scarf I'd dropped in the forest, what felt like a lifetime ago. My fingers curled around the cloth, and I hugged it to my chest as if it could somehow bring back what was lost.

'What's the story there?' he asked quietly, his tone softer than before.

I clutched the scarf with both hands, inhaling the faint scent of honey still clinging to the fabric. It brought back memories—sweet, fleeting, and now unbearably painful. 'One that never got to start,' I whispered, the words almost lost in the weight of my grief.

He watched me, his expression inscrutable. 'I'm sorry.'

I shook my head, blinking away the tears that blurred my vision. 'I'm tired,' I muttered. 'I'm going to rest. Wake me when we arrive. And I better see my sister when we do.'

'You will,' he promised.

I turned away from him, pressing my forehead against the cool glass of the carriage window. Tears finally spilled over, hot and relentless, burning a path down my cheeks. My throat tightened with a pain so fierce it felt like my heart was caged, threatening to shatter with every breath.

Outside, the world passed in a blur, but all I could feel was the agony lodged deep within my chest—the hollow ache of loss that refused to let go.

And in the darkness of the carriage, with nothing but the sound of the wheels and the silence between us, I let myself cry.

* * *

I was floating—no, walking—through an endless expanse of golden light, where the air felt alive, breathing with me. The world around me was soft and warm, humming with a quiet song I couldn't quite place. Each step I took made the ground ripple as if it were made of water and sunlight.

In the distance, I saw a figure—steady, solid, unmistakably Kal.

My heart stirred, a mix of relief and apprehension. Kal always carried a quiet power, a gravity that pulled everything into focus. He stood there, motionless but not idle, as if waiting. Patient. Sure. And suddenly, I wasn't sure I was ready. What if I disrupt his calm with my chaos? What if I ruin the perfect stillness of this moment?

But something in me moved forward anyway. I was drawn to him like a tide to the shore. As I got closer, Kal turned, his face soft with a calm understanding that made my chest ache. There was no judgment, no hesitation—just him, open and steady, as if he'd been waiting for me all along.

'Mel,' he said, his voice low and grounding, and for a moment, it felt like the whole world paused to listen.

I wanted to say something back—anything—but words wouldn't come. Instead, I reached for his hand, and when our fingers touched, a spark ignited in the air around us. The light shifted, swirling into a kaleidoscope of colours, and suddenly we were standing in a vast forest. The trees glowed faintly, their leaves shimmering like silver in the soft breeze. It felt alive, vibrant, and endless. Yet somehow, it didn't overwhelm me. Kal's hand remained in mine, anchoring me.

We walked together, not saying much, but it didn't feel like silence. Every step felt deliberate as if we were creating something with each movement. I glanced at Kal, and he was looking ahead, focused but calm. His presence steadied me, and for the first time in a long while, I didn't feel the need to fill the quiet.

We reached a clearing where a lake stretched out before us, impossibly still, reflecting the stars and the glowing trees around us. Kal knelt beside the water and looked up at me. I hesitated, unsure of what to do, but he nodded, encouraging me. Slowly, I knelt too, gazing into the lake.

The reflection staring back surprised me. It wasn't just me—it was us. Our images blurred, overlapping as if the lake couldn't tell where one of us ended and the other began. My throat tightened. I felt vulnerable and exposed. But Kal didn't let go of my hand. He squeezed it gently, reminding me I wasn't alone.

'I...' My voice cracked, and I looked away, but Kal didn't rush me. The reflection shifted, and I saw something else now—a balance. His calm steadied my fire. My energy stirred his quiet strength. Together, we weren't chaotic or broken. We were whole.

And then I heard it—the melody. Soft at first, but growing with every heartbeat. It was familiar yet new as if it had always been inside me, waiting to be found. I started to hum, and Kal watched me with a small, almost reverent smile. The melody wove itself around us, filling the clearing and echoing through the forest. It wasn't just my song any more. It was ours.

Kal pulled me to my feet, and we stood there, facing the lake, the forest, and the infinite stars above. For the first time in what felt like forever, I wasn't afraid. I was just here, with Kal, in this perfect, unspoken harmony.

And then the dream faded, the melody lingering like a whispered promise.

I woke with my tears still running, my heart full of an ache that felt as though it would never leave.

II

Part Two

Friendly Fae and Feral Family

Twenty-Five

Aria

The camp wasn't much to look at—a scattering of tents pitched unevenly across a clearing, their fabric weathered and patched from years of use. The smell of damp earth and smouldering wood hung in the air, mingling with the sharp tang of cold steel and the faint, sweet aroma of the forest beyond. Everything here felt temporary, fragile, as if it might disappear with the next gust of wind.

Men and women moved with quiet efficiency, their faces etched with fatigue and guarded determination. They were fighters, survivors, but the wear of endless conflict showed in the way their shoulders slumped when they thought no one was watching. A few lingered near the campfire at the centre, their laughter low and brittle, as though they were trying to remember what joy felt like.

To the west, horses were tethered to crude wooden posts, their breath fogging in the crisp evening air. Beyond them, supply wagons groaned under the weight of provisions and weapons, their wheels caked with mud. The distant sound of sharpening blades cut through the stillness, a reminder that no matter how quiet the night seemed, war was never far away.

It wasn't home—nothing about it felt safe or certain. But there was a strange kind of comfort in its imperfection, in the camaraderie of shared struggle. This camp wasn't just a place to rest; it was a lifeline, a fleeting sanctuary where we could catch our breath before facing the storm again.

* * *

'Please,' I begged, looking up at Verno with wide eyes. He stood there, arms crossed, unmoved.

'No. You two together could start trouble,' he said, his tone curt.

'I promise,' I pleaded, stepping closer. 'I swear we won't do anything. Just let us see each other—just for one night.'

He sighed heavily, considering. Then, with a reluctant nod, he held out his pinky. 'One night only.'

A grin broke through my desperation as I hooked my pinky with his. 'One night only, I promise.'

He shook his head, clearly regretting this already. 'Fine. Hurry up, then.'

I turned and sprinted, skirts flying as I called out, 'Mel!'

'Aria?' Melody rushed in, arms open wide, and I all but crashed into her embrace.

'You're staying?' Mel asked, eyeing Verno warily.

'Of course I'm staying,' Verno muttered.

'The two of you are—'

'Chaotic,' I finished for him.

'Funny?' Melody suggested.

'Cute?' I teased.

'Horrific,' she laughed, eyes twinkling.

The general's lips quirked. 'Dangerous,' he said firmly, a dark edge to his voice. 'Downright dangerous.'

Melody cupped my face, her fingers gentle against my skin. 'Will you be okay on your own?' she asked, her eyes searching mine. 'You know, if you want, I'll light them all up. I'll kill them for you.'

I shook my head, whispering, 'No, Mel. I don't want that. We're safe here. For now.'

'Safe?' She scoffed, glancing around the dimly lit tent. 'Don't be stupid. Don't trust them, no matter how much his smile makes your heart flutter.'

'Mel, I'm engaged,' I muttered, casting a wary glance at the general as he unfastened his heavy black cloak, revealing a simple white shirt underneath.

'So?' she replied softly, her voice whispering in the wind.

I shook my head, trying to refocus. 'How are you holding up with… everything?'

Melody's expression grew distant. 'I'm handling it,' she said, voice steady. 'It's not like I'm a stranger to death.'

'Mel…'

'I don't say it to be pitied.' She looked down, her voice a whisper. 'It's just… a fact.' She cleared her throat and lifted her chin, taking both my hands in hers. 'Grieving is one of my greatest skills, and I'll pass through the ugly steps to acceptance.'

'So you're not blaming yourself? Not angry? Not… sad?'

She shook her head. 'No, I'm not. And I'm not losing control of my powers either.'

'I didn't say—'

'It's okay,' she cut me off gently. 'You're worried, and I get it. I would be too.' Her eyebrows furrowed in that familiar way that always made my heart twist. 'How about you? Your heart's softer than mine. You care about every soul, even if they are strangers. I know you'll cry for weeks.'

I swallowed, my throat tight. 'I do feel… guilty. And sad. It's just so unfair. Those bandits should pay for what they did.'

A dark smile flickered across Mel's lips. 'Oh, they did.'

I stiffened. 'What do you mean, Mel?'

Her mouth clamped shut, but the truth was already there, hanging between us. 'Mel, did you or did you not… kill someone?' I pressed, arms crossed, the silence between us growing heavier.

She hesitated, then muttered, 'No, well, perhaps.'

I stared at her. 'The leader?'

Her eyes darkened. 'He saved us because he wanted to… use me,' she spat, her voice rising. From the corner of my eye, I saw the general's head snap up, his attention now fully on us. I pulled Mel aside, away from his gaze.

'His lust saved us,' she continued, her voice dropping to a cold whisper. 'They killed our friends. They killed Kal. Of course, they were going to die.' Her tone was so devoid of emotion that it sent a chill through me. In moments like this, I was reminded why she was truly our father's daughter.

She looked at me, her voice a venomous whisper. 'If it were my choice, they would have all been tortured for years for what they did.'

Twenty-Six

Melody

❧

'Sit.' His voice was calm but carried the authority of someone who was used to being obeyed.

I lowered myself onto the floor beside him, eyeing the lavish spread of fruits and dishes that covered the table. Food that, until now, I had forgotten existed.

'Wine?' he offered, pouring a glass without waiting for my answer.

'I don't drink,' I replied shortly.

He nodded, unfazed, and gestured to the food. 'Then eat.'

I let out a soft scoff despite myself.

'What?' His gaze sharpened, studying me with an intensity I couldn't ignore.

'Nothing.'

'Say it.'

'Why are you being nice?' I asked, crossing my arms. 'Why are we even alive?'

He set his glass down, meeting my gaze steadily. 'What do you mean?'

'My sister and I are heirs to the throne you claim to want so badly. Why keep us alive if it's power you're after?'

'Because I don't wish for war.'

I let out a bitter chuckle. 'That isn't true. You want war with my father.'

'You forget your bloodline,' he said, his tone firm but strangely respectful. 'You're Fae—noble Fae, even. You and your sister are direct descendants of the third Fae bloodline.'

I couldn't help but laugh, my tone cutting. 'Ah, so you don't wish to disrupt the peace in your own kingdom.'

His expression softened, and for a moment, he almost looked sincere. 'I refuse to harm you or your sister. The three bloodlines have lived in harmony for centuries. My father was a friend to your mother and grandmother—and perhaps even your ancestors. Your aunt helped me secure my throne. Even High Queen Lethe blessed me.'

'And yet,' I countered, 'we've never met. The King of the Dark Fae was rumoured to be old and heirless.'

'Evidently, that was a lie,' he said, a smirk playing at his lips.

'I thought Fae were immortal.'

'We are, but we're not invincible. My father was killed by a soldier in war.'

'We are not at war with the Dark Fae!' I shot back, disbelief lacing my voice.

He rolled his eyes. 'Really, Melody, do you think your father earned his nickname purely because of how he treats you? No. He is *mad*.'

The words landed heavily. Of course, my father never told me of things happening at court or in the other kingdoms. But a war? Anger pulsed through me at the betrayal.

I leaned forward slightly, curiosity mingling with caution. 'Why keep your existence a secret? You know my mother wished for alliances through marriage. If you wanted my throne so badly, you could have had it.'

'Through marriage?' He raised an eyebrow, swirling his glass. 'Would that not create a ruler too powerful, holding two kingdoms?'

'It has been done before,' I replied, meeting his gaze.

'With a regent in one kingdom.' He studied me carefully. 'Would you give up your crown?'

'Never.'

He laughed, clinking his glass in a silent toast. 'Exactly.'

'And what of Aria?' I pressed. 'You could have married her, even if you are a bastard king.'

His eyes flickered, but his voice remained steady. 'Like you said, a bastard king. I have no claim on your sister. She remains untouched by these politics.'

I narrowed my gaze. 'So what's your plan, then?'

He leaned back, relaxed but attentive. 'I will deliver you both safely to your aunt's court.'

'My aunt knows of your plans; I take it?'

'Yes,' he replied simply.

'And her alliance with my father?'

'She cares little for what happens to him,' he said, his tone devoid of sympathy. 'Her concern is for you.'

I scoffed. 'Nice to know I have some protection somewhere.'

He shrugged, a faint smile softening his features. 'Rest easy. I promise you won't be harmed here.'

I studied him carefully, my suspicion evident. 'You aren't fully Fae, are you?'

He met my gaze, unflinching. 'No, I'm not.'

I shook my head softly. 'Then I won't trust your words.'

He smiled, almost approvingly. 'I wouldn't expect anything less.' He gestured at my plate with his knife. 'Now, eat.'

I returned his smile with a reluctant eye roll and began to cut into the steak, letting the rich juices pool around the edges of my plate.

The meal felt like a delicate negotiation—every bite a reminder that, for now, we both had something to gain by keeping the peace.

Twenty-Seven

Aria

❦

'You need to control your powers,' Verno said, his voice steady but stern as he surveyed the ice spreading across the floor.

'I'm sorry,' I gasped, my breath hitching. Frost crept beneath my feet. 'I was just... thinking of my fiancé. He'll be furious to know another man has slept in the same tent as me.'

Verno's eyes flickered with interest. 'Your fiancé?'

'Yes,' I muttered, more to myself than to him. 'He will find me.'

He cocked his head, studying me. 'Is he truly your knight in shining armour?'

I nodded, but my voice wavered. 'Yes.'

His eyes sharpened as he stepped closer, his presence unnervingly calm. 'Then why is there fear in your voice?' He reached out, tilting my chin up to meet his gaze. His eyes searched mine. 'Most girls speak of their lovers with hope, with joy. You, however… you speak of him as though it's a fate you're trying to escape.'

A shiver ran through me. 'I… I cannot escape him,' I whispered.

'Do you *wish* to?' His question was soft, almost tender.

'He loves me,' I insisted, the words tumbling out. 'He loves me the best way he knows how. It's the only way I've ever seen love.'

Verno's eyes narrowed. 'But is it the kind of love you want?'

Frustration flared, and I pushed him away. 'Stop filling my head with this nonsense.'

'Nonsense?' he repeated, his tone infuriatingly calm.

'Yes!' I shouted, snowflakes swirling from my hands in erratic bursts. 'I love him.'

'Why?'

'What?' I stared at him, thrown by the simplicity of his question.

'Tell me why you love him,' he pressed, voice quiet but insistent.

I hesitated, searching for an answer. 'Because… he will be my husband. He brings me beautiful jewellery, he arranges my things just how I like them, and he is… decent.'

Verno's laugh was low and mocking. 'That's what you call love? Trinkets and neat arrangements?'

I took a step forward, ice crackling beneath my feet. 'He's attractive, and he makes my heart race. I get butterflies waiting for his replies. Yes, we have problems, but we'll work through them. We'll compromise. As long as I have his heart, nothing else matters.'

Verno leaned in closer, his voice a soft whisper against my ear. 'So it's lust, then? You crave his touch.'

'No!' I blurted, too quickly, too defensively. 'It's… it's more than that.'

His gaze was unrelenting. 'Has he even touched you enough for you to know?'

I hesitated, my voice dropping to a whisper. 'He hasn't… touched me enough for me to be certain.'

Verno nodded slowly. 'Okay,' he said simply, stepping back, leaving me with my thoughts.

Before I could respond, Jas entered, a vision of elegance draped in soft pink silk, her outfit adorned with silver jewels that glittered under the torchlight. The scarf covering her hair flowed gracefully as she moved.

'You look beautiful,' I said, a bit envious of her composed grace.

She laughed softly. 'Thank you. I try.'

'How do you always manage to look so put together?' I asked, glancing down at my own wrinkled clothes.

'A lifetime of living in caves teaches you to be prepared,' she replied with a wink. 'I knew we'd be on the move, so I packed well.'

'Do you have your own tent?'

'Yes,' she said with a proud smile. 'It even has a table and chair. Honey, I'm like you.'

I tilted my head. 'Like me?'

'Royalty.' She grinned, taking my hand. 'My brother was the King of Thieves, and he earned that name for good reason. We may have been a wandering tribe, but I still have people who depend on me.'

I nodded, letting her words sink in. 'But… not the men on this journey?'

Her smile faltered. 'Not these men, no. My brother brought

only his most trusted circle. They would never have accepted me.'

'So you saved us… for your brother's throne?'

Jas's fingers brushed through my hair gently. 'In a way,' she admitted. 'But I saved so many more lives than just yours.'

I sighed as she continued to fiddle with my hair. 'You don't struggle with death?'

Her eyes grew thoughtful. 'War isn't something you consider? Your mother was said to be a great warrior.'

I shrugged. 'I would rather never see war. I want peace.'

Jas laughed, her tone softening. 'Ah, a pacifist. That must be why you were born second.'

I turned to look at her, slightly offended.

'No disrespect, my dear,' she added quickly, 'but you seem like the perfect princess. Being queen would destroy your gentle soul. And there's nothing wrong with that. Not everyone is meant for the throne, for the ugly politics of war.'

'You think so?' I asked, searching her eyes for sincerity.

She nodded. 'Yes. What is your greatest dream?'

I paused, taken aback. 'My dream?'

'Yes, sweetie. Your dream.'

I smiled softly, allowing myself to indulge in a rare moment of honesty. 'To ride a horse through the meadows as the sun shines above me, to swim in natural pools… to do nothing at all, but with someone who truly loves me.' I laughed, the thought almost silly amidst the chaos of my current life.

Jas's eyes softened, and she squeezed my hand. 'That is a beautiful dream. And I truly hope you get it.'

'Thank you,' I whispered, turning my gaze back toward the tent's opening, where I could see Verno outside, talking with Aladin. The sound of their laughter drifted in, and I couldn't help but smile at the sight.

But that smile faded quickly as a troubling realization gnawed at my heart.

The thoughts and dreams that were starting to take root in my mind… they were dangerous.

Very dangerous.

Twenty-Eight

Melody

'What the hell are you doing? Get out!' I shouted, my voice sharp with frustration.

'No, I'm tired,' Damion replied nonchalantly. 'And I wish to rest now.'

'I'm changing!' I snapped, struggling to keep my voice steady.

'There's a privacy screen,' he said, waving a hand dismissively.

'You can still see my damn shadow,' I shot back.

He smirked, the expression infuriating. 'Darling, I'm not looking.'

I scoffed, yanking my dress off behind the screen. 'As if that makes me feel safe.'

His voice softened, losing some of its usual edge. 'I would never touch you, or even look, without your consent.'

I froze for a moment, pulling the gown over my shoulders. The anger simmering beneath my skin didn't fade. 'I don't believe you,' I said flatly.

'Why?' he asked, his tone genuinely curious.

'Because that's how the world works,' I muttered, bitterness creeping into my voice.

There was a beat of silence before he replied, gentler than I expected. 'I will allow you your privacy to dress. This one time.'

'Okay.'

The silence that followed felt thick, and heavy with unspoken tension. Finally, I poked my head out from behind the screen, glaring at him.

'What? You expect me to thank you for basic decency?'

He chuckled, turning his back to me. 'I'll take my leave and return to sleep.'

I stepped out, the soft fabric of the gown brushing against my skin. 'I'm done,' I said, arms crossed as I faced him.

He turned, his eyes briefly sweeping over me before meeting my gaze. 'I'm not letting you and your sister sleep in your tent again.'

'Why not?'

'Your thoughts are dangerous when you're together,' he said simply, as though it were an indisputable fact.

I scoffed, annoyance prickling. 'Can I ask you something?'

He nodded. 'Yes.'

'You're a witch, not just Fae, aren't you?'

His eyes glimmered with something unreadable. 'Close.'

I rolled my eyes at his answer. 'Then why do you cling to your Father's power so closely? Why not your Mother's?'

He tilted his head, considering my question. 'I haven't inherited my Mother's *gifts*... yet.'

He extended his hand as if to demonstrate. The air shifted, coalescing into a shape that solidified with a whisper. A crimson rose bloomed in his palm.

I laughed, taking the rose from him. 'I can do that too, easily.'

'But you don't,' he said, his gaze lingering. 'You love your thorns, but you ignore the roses.'

I shrugged, lowering myself onto the mattress across from him. 'I like my Fatal power. Is that so wrong?'

Damion leaned forward, his eyes narrowing slightly. 'Perhaps not. But why do you deny the beauty of your roses?'

'They're useless,' I said with a dismissive wave. 'I enjoy the thorns. They're what people fear.'

He smiled faintly. 'But roses are what your people love. I've heard tales of the shows you put on for your court—letting roses bloom in intricate designs.'

I rolled my eyes. 'That was just for show.'

'And your sister?' he asked, his curiosity deepening. 'What of her powers?'

'She doesn't like to use them,' I replied curtly.

'Interesting,' he murmured, studying me. Then he straightened, his calm demeanour slipping back into place. 'Very well. Now, go sleep on the floor.'

I raised an eyebrow. 'You think I'll take orders so easily?'

A lazy grin spread across his lips. 'I am a king, after all. Did you really think I'd gift you the royal tent?' He strolled away, pulling back a curtain to reveal a raised bed adorned with silks and pillows.

I groaned in frustration as he called out over his shoulder, 'Good night.'

Left alone, I stood there for a moment, feeling the cool air against my skin. The scent of the rose he'd conjured lingered in my hands, its softness a stark contrast to the icy thorns I was used to wielding.

But as I watched him disappear behind the curtain, I couldn't help but wonder…

Maybe he was right. Maybe there was something more I could wield than just fear.

Something that was far more dangerous.

And that, perhaps, terrified me most of all.

* * *

I woke from yet another dream of the love that never came to life. Quietly, I sneaked out of the tent, my bare feet pressing into the cool grass. The campsite was impossibly still, like the world was holding its breath.

My knees sank into the damp ground as I cried softly, my fingers clutching the scarf he left behind. It was so soft, softer than I remembered, but the faint scent of cedar and citrus was fading. I buried my face in it, trying to inhale what was left.

He's gone.

The words tasted bitter in my mind, jagged and impossible to swallow. I didn't know how to exist in a world without him. Everything felt smaller and dimmer. The air was heavy in my lungs like it didn't want me to breathe any more.

'You promised,' I whispered into the emptiness, my voice breaking. I didn't know if I was saying it to him, to myself, or to the silence.

I closed my eyes, hoping to see him—his crooked smile, the way his eyes crinkled when he laughed. For a moment, I almost could. But when I opened my eyes, it was just me.

The scarf slipped from my fingers, pooling in my lap. A sob escaped before I could stop it, raw and ugly, and I pressed my hand to my mouth to muffle the sound. But it kept coming, wave after wave, until I was gasping, clutching at the empty air like I might catch him, like I might pull him back.

The night was the only time I could grieve, the only time I could think of him without prying eyes. Damion could never see me like this, so broken.

The rain began to fall steadily, its soft rhythm tapping against the ground. I tilted my head to the sky, letting it soak through my hair, my gown. I stared up at the dark clouds, my chest heaving, and wondered if the sky was mourning too. If it cried because it knew what I'd lost.

I let the rain wash over me, crawling all around, dragging my tears into the earth.

But the rain would stop. It always did.

And when it did, I would still be here, in the silence, without him.

Twenty-Nine

Aria

'I wish to return home.' My voice was soft, almost a whisper.

Melody turned to me, her eyes narrowing. 'Do you really? And why would you want that?'

I hesitated. 'Because Father is—'

'Oh, who cares?' she interrupted, her tone dripping with exasperation.

'What?' I stared at her, taken aback.

She crossed her arms, eyes blazing. 'Aria, wasn't it you who wanted to marry just to gain freedom?'

'Yes, but—'

'Look around you!' She gestured to the open expanse beyond our tent. 'We're free now.'

I shook my head. 'We're not free, Mel. We're prisoners.'

'Prisoners?' She laughed, though there was no joy in it. 'We're far less imprisoned than we ever were at court.'

'Mel, I won't stay here,' I insisted, my voice hardening.

She shrugged a casual dismissal. 'Then don't.' But then her voice dropped to a whisper, her eyes darkening.

'You do realize it's your throne he wants, right? Your crown. You've perfected your magic, played their twisted games of politics, made a spectacle of yourself—for what? To just hand it all over to him?' I said.

I met her gaze, steady and unflinching. 'Will you really not fight for what's yours?'

She stared at the ground, her voice barely audible. 'I… I enjoy being free.'

'No, Mel. That's not true.' I stepped closer, forcing her to meet my eyes. 'You've never truly wanted freedom.'

Her eyes flashed with defiance. 'That's not true!'

'You love our home,' I insisted, my voice softening.

She shook her head violently. 'No, I loved *Kal*,' she shouted, the rawness in her voice startling me. 'And he's dead.' Her voice broke, and she turned away, her shoulders trembling. 'So, no—I see no reason to go back.'

I let out a bitter laugh. 'And you think I have one? Do you think I'm eager to marry a man I don't love?'

Mel's eyes widened, a flicker of confusion. 'But wasn't that your dream?'

I shook my head, tears burning at the back of my eyes. 'I thought it was… but I've realized it was just survival. My real dream is to be free. But you,' I took her hands in mine, 'your dream has always been to be queen.'

Her voice trembled. 'You would sacrifice your dream for mine?'

I nodded, squeezing her hands. 'Don't you get it, Mel? You are as much my sister as I am yours. There's nothing I wouldn't do for you. I will find my freedom once you sit on that throne.'

She pulled her hands back, shaking her head. 'Can't we just return after he's... gone?'

'Father's?' I stared at her, shocked. 'How can you even say that?'

She bit her lip, her eyes filled with a desperate, pleading look. 'Must we endure a war?'

'He's family, Mel!' I shouted, fury rising in my chest. 'We are his daughters, his greatest warriors. We cannot stand by and let him die.'

'I know,' she said, voice barely a whisper. 'But—'

'But nothing!' I cut her off, my voice trembling with rage. 'His death is not something I will even entertain discussing.'

Without waiting for her reply, I turned on my heel and stormed away, my heart pounding in my chest.

The sound of my sister's quiet sobs echoed behind me, but I forced myself not to look back. For both our sakes, I had to stay resolute.

* * *

The meadow was coated in my frost, shimmering faintly under the pale light of the afternoon sun. My breath curled in the air like smoke as I paced, my boots crunching softly against the frozen grass. Everything felt too still, the cold too sharp, as if the world itself were waiting for me to mess this up.

Verno leaned against a tree nearby, his arms crossed and his expression unreadable. His calmness irritated me almost as much as his insistence that this was the best place to practice.

'I don't know why you think this is going to work,' I said, scowling at him. 'Last time I tried, I nearly froze an entire room—and that was indoors.'

'Exactly,' he said, pushing off the tree and walking toward me. 'Out here, there's nothing to hurt. No one to hurt. Just you, your magic, and space to figure it out.'

I hesitated, the weight of his words pressing against the doubt that churned in my chest. My magic wasn't some gentle thing. It was wild, sharp, and cold. It left frost on my skin and shards of ice in my wake. I'd spent years pretending it wasn't there, hoping it would just disappear.

But it hadn't. And now I had no choice but to face it.

'What if I can't control it?' I asked, my voice quieter now. 'What if I make things worse?'

Verno's gaze softened. 'Then I'll stop you,' he said simply, as if it were the most obvious thing in the world.

'How?' I asked, narrowing my eyes. 'You can't exactly punch a snowstorm into submission.'

His lips quirked into a faint smile. 'No, but I'm resourceful. And I trust you.'

'Trusting me seems like a mistake,' I muttered.

'Trusting you,' he said, his tone firm, 'is the smartest thing I've done in a long time.'

Something about the way he said it made my chest tighten. I looked away, focusing on the frost-covered meadow. 'Fine. Let's get this over with.'

Thirty

Melody

Jaz frowned down at me, her hands on her hips, clearly exasperated. 'Come on, Rose.'

I clenched my jaw. 'It's Mel.'

She blinked, then sighed, waving it off. 'Yes, sorry. I forget sometimes. But listen, Aladin won't hurt you.'

I shifted my gaze to Aladin, who stood a few steps away, watching us with a wary expression. 'I'm sorry,' I said, though my tone was anything but apologetic. 'But I don't trust you. I promise I'm fine.'

Jaz crossed her arms, frustration deepening the lines around her eyes. 'What is the problem, then?'

'She still refuses to let me heal her,' Aladin muttered under his breath, his dark eyes flicking between us.

Damion, who had been silently observing, snapped to attention. 'Leave, Aladin.' His voice was low and dangerous.

Aladin's eyes widened, but he nodded, turning to leave

with Jaz trailing behind him. Neither looked back as they disappeared through the tent flaps.

I let out a breath I didn't realize I was holding, but Damion's gaze was now fixed on me, piercing. 'Why do you refuse the healer?'

I met his eyes defiantly. 'I don't trust him.'

'Yet you allowed him to treat your sister,' he said, voice tight with frustration.

'That's because I was there,' I shot back. 'I could have slit his throat if necessary. Besides, she needed him.'

Damion's eyes narrowed. 'And you don't?'

'I do not.'

He let out a harsh laugh. 'I saw—'

'I *knew* you looked!' I interrupted, my face flushing with anger. How dare he? A small piece of my heart broke as I realized my betrayal to Kal. It had been merely a month, and already I was allowing another to look at me?

'I didn't mean to.' His voice softened slightly, but his eyes stayed locked on mine. 'But it doesn't matter. You need healing.'

'Sit down.'

'No.' I crossed my arms, refusing to yield.

His jaw clenched, and his voice dropped to a growl. 'Now. I won't repeat myself.'

Reluctantly, I sat down on the edge of the mattress, my arms still wrapped protectively around myself. 'Fine. What now?'

He stepped closer, so close I could feel the heat radiating from him. 'Take off your top.'

My eyes widened. 'Excuse me?'

'I am a healer,' he said, his voice steady.

'You're a king,' I countered, my tone sharp and rising like wildfire.

He tilted his head, almost amused. 'A Fae king, yes. But we all learn the skills of a healer.'

I glared at him. 'What makes you think I trust you any more than I trusted him?'

'Nothing.' He leaned in, his gaze unwavering. 'But I'm not giving you a choice.'

'Wow.' The sarcasm dripped from my voice, but he ignored it.

His hands were surprisingly gentle as they pressed against my cold skin, warmth flooding into me where he touched. Despite myself, I shivered, the heat from his palms thawing the icy tension within me.

'This might hurt,' he warned softly.

'What might—' I barely finished the question before a sharp sting made me gasp. 'Fuck!' I hissed, wincing as he rubbed something into a cut I hadn't realized was there.

I stumbled forward from the pain, but he caught me, one arm wrapping firmly around my waist to steady me.

'I'm fine,' I muttered, though I could feel my legs trembling.

'Are you sure?' His breath was warm against my ear, his arm still holding me close.

'Yes.' I nodded quickly, trying to ignore the strange flutter in my chest.

'Good.' He slowly released me, but his hand lingered at my waist, a touch that was almost… tender. 'Now, close your eyes and rest. The pain will ease if you sleep through it.'

I nodded reluctantly, my body betraying me as exhaustion crept back in. 'Okay,' I whispered, letting him guide me back down onto the mattress. The moment my head hit the pillow, my eyes drifted shut.

Aria

I closed my eyes, taking a deep breath. The cold was always there, just beneath the surface of my skin, a second heartbeat that pulsed with icy precision. It was sharp and restless, and I'd spent so long trying to lock it away that even thinking about it made me uneasy.

'Start small,' Verno said behind me. 'Don't try to control it all at once. Just let it come to you.'

I let out a slow breath, focusing on the cold in my chest. It stirred, tentative, as if it weren't sure whether to trust me. Slowly, I extended my hands, palms up, and reached for it. At first, nothing happened. Then I felt it—a whisper of frost curling around my fingertips.

When I opened my eyes, tiny snowflakes swirled in the air above my palms. They glimmered faintly, delicate and fragile, as if they might melt at any moment.

'You're doing it,' Verno said softly, his voice closer now.

I smiled, a flicker of pride warming me despite the cold. 'It's... beautiful.'

'It is,' he said, though when I glanced at him, his eyes weren't on the snowflakes—they were on me.

The thought sent my focus spiraling, and the snowflakes turned sharp, their edges hardening into shards of ice. They spun faster, the air growing colder around us. Panic surged in my chest, and the frost spread across the ground, creeping toward the trees.

'Aria!' Verno's voice cut through the rising chaos. 'You're in control. Focus!'

'I can't—' My voice broke as the ice flared, sharp and jagged. The magic was slipping away from me, spiraling into something I couldn't contain.

'Yes, you can.' He stepped closer, his hands steady as he reached for mine. 'Breathe. Look at me.'

I forced myself to meet his gaze. His dark eyes were calm, steady, grounding me in a way I didn't expect. Slowly, I mirrored his breathing, the rise and fall of his chest syncing with mine.

The frost began to recede, the shards of ice softening into snow once more. The air grew lighter, the biting chill easing until it was just cold enough to sting my cheeks. The snowflakes swirled lazily around us, weightless and peaceful.

'There,' Verno said softly, his hands still hovering near mine. 'You did it.'

I stared at the snowflakes, wonder and disbelief warring in my chest. 'I... I did.'

'You're stronger than you think,' he said, a faint smile tugging at his lips. 'You just need to trust yourself.'

I glanced at him, my heart still racing. 'How are you not afraid of me?'

'Because I know you,' he said simply. 'And because I've seen what you can do when you stop doubting yourself.'

For a moment, I couldn't speak. The weight of his words settled over me, and I realized he wasn't just talking about my magic. He believed in me—in all of me. The thought was as terrifying as it was comforting.

'Thank you,' I said finally, my voice barely above a whisper.

'Anytime,' he said, his smile softening. 'Ready to try again?'

I looked at the snowflakes dancing around us, then back at him. 'Yeah,' I said, a small smile tugging at my lips. 'I think I am.'

And as I reached for the magic again, this time, it felt less like a battle and more like a dance.

The snowflakes swirled lazily in the air, shimmering like tiny stars against the golden afternoon light. My chest heaved as I lowered my hands, the magic receding gently now, like a tide pulling back from the shore. I couldn't stop staring at the frost-covered meadow, at the tiny crystalline structures glinting on the grass. Proof that I had done it.

I had controlled it.

My hands still trembled, not from fear, but from exhilaration. For the first time in years, I didn't feel like my magic was something to be feared. It was something to be understood, something to be embraced.

'It's… beautiful,' I murmured, more to myself than to Verno.

'You did that,' he said, his voice steady and warm. 'Not the magic. You.'

I turned to look at him, my heart catching in my chest. There was pride in his eyes, but more than that—there was belief. A kind of unwavering faith I hadn't seen in anyone else, not even myself. It was too much, and yet, it wasn't enough.

Without thinking, I stepped forward and wrapped my arms around him.

For a moment, he froze. I could feel the surprise in the way his body tensed, his breath hitching slightly. But then his arms came around me, strong and steady, grounding me in a way I didn't know I needed. The warmth of his embrace chased away the lingering chill, and I closed my eyes, letting myself sink into the moment.

'Thank you,' I whispered against his shoulder, my voice trembling. 'For not giving up on me.'

'I never will,' he said softly, his breath warm against my hair. 'Not ever.'

It was such a simple promise, and yet it hit me harder than anything else. I held onto him a little tighter, afraid to let go, as if breaking the moment would shatter the fragile peace I'd found.

'Am I interrupting?'

The voice made me pull back sharply, my cheeks burning as I turned to see Melody standing at the edge of the meadow. Her arms were crossed, her brow arched, but her expression was unreadable. She wasn't smiling, but she wasn't glaring either.

I stepped back from Verno, suddenly acutely aware of how close we'd been. 'Melody,' I said quickly, trying to keep my voice steady. 'I was just—'

'Practicing?' she interrupted, her tone light but edged with curiosity. Her gaze flicked to Verno, then back to me. 'Looked like more than that.'

'It's not what it looks like,' I said, though even I wasn't sure what I meant by that.

Verno, of course, didn't seem remotely fazed. 'She did it,' he said, his voice calm as he gestured to the frost-covered meadow. 'She controlled it.'

Melody's expression softened, and a small, genuine smile tugged at her lips. 'You did?' she asked, her gaze shifting to me.

I nodded, still a little breathless. 'Yeah. I did.'

'That's amazing, Aria.' Her smile widened, pride coloring her voice. But her gaze flicked back to Verno for a split second, and I could tell she wasn't entirely sure what to make of him.

'I just… needed a little help,' I said, glancing at him. He gave me a small, almost imperceptible nod, and for a moment, it felt like we were sharing a secret.

'Well,' Melody said after a pause, her tone playful now. 'If you're done freezing the meadow, Damion's looking for us. Something about needing a strategy for when we get to the Fae Kingdom.'

'Of course he is,' Verno muttered, earning a soft laugh from Melody.

She turned, her cloak swirling behind her, and started walking back toward the camp. Verno waited until she was out of earshot before glancing at me.

'You okay?' he asked, his voice quieter now.

'Yeah,' I said, offering him a small smile. 'I think I am.'

His lips quirked into a faint grin. 'Good. Because this is just the beginning.'

I watched him walk toward the camp, his confident stride leaving footprints in the frost, and for the first time, I felt something new—something terrifying but undeniably real.

I wasn't sure what it was yet. But I knew it had everything to do with Verno.

* * *

The voices were still ringing in my ears as I tried to steady my breath, leaning against the cool, rough fabric of the tent wall. The conversation with Verno kept replaying in my mind— his hands on my skin, the unexpected warmth of his touch, the way his eyes had lingered just a second too long. I forced those thoughts away. Now was not the time to be distracted by emotions that had no place here.

Mel's voice cut through my muddled thoughts, sharper than a knife. 'Have you completely lost your mind?'

I looked up to see her standing at the entrance of the tent, eyes blazing, arms crossed tightly over her chest.

'What now?' I sighed, pushing myself away from the wall.

'You're letting him get close,' she accused, her tone filled with the kind of hurt that only comes from someone who cares too much. 'He's the reason our friends are dead. How can you forget that?'

I clenched my teeth, fighting the urge to scream. 'I haven't forgotten.'

'Could have fooled me,' she muttered, stepping closer. 'You trust him enough to let him touch you, to heal you. But where was that mercy when our people needed it? When they were crying for help?'

Her words struck deep, reopening wounds I thought I had buried. 'You think I don't remember their screams?' I hissed.

A cold silence settled between us. I could see the pain in her eyes, but there was something else there too. Fear. Fear that I was slipping, that I was letting my guard down.

'I'm not falling for him,' I said, my voice wavering despite myself.

Mel's gaze didn't soften. If anything, it grew harder. 'Aren't you?'

I shook my head, but even as I did, my mind betrayed me with flashes of Verno's eyes, the way they seemed to pierce right through me. 'He's just a friend,' I insisted, but the words felt hollow, even to me.

She stepped closer, her voice dropping to a whisper. 'Do you truly believe that? Or is it just easier to pretend?'

I couldn't meet her eyes. I couldn't face the truth she was trying to force out of me. Instead, I turned away, clenching my fists to stop my hands from shaking. 'Yes,' I whispered. 'He's just a friend.'

Mel let out a soft, bitter laugh. 'Then perhaps you should remind yourself. Because it's starting to look like something far more dangerous.'

The weight of her words hung in the air, choking me. I wanted to argue, to lash out, to defend myself, but all I could think about was Verno's touch, his quiet intensity, the way he looked at me as if he could see all the parts of me I tried to hide.

And the most terrifying part?

I was starting to wish he would never stop looking.

As Mel turned to leave, her steps heavy with disappointment, I was left alone in the dim light of the tent. My hands shook, the aftermath of the confrontation leaving me feeling hollow.

What was happening to me? I sank onto the edge of the mattress, my mind racing. How could I be so foolish as to even entertain the idea that Verno could be anything more than an enemy?

Yet, in the quiet moments when it was just the two of us, I couldn't help but feel something stir deep within me. A warmth, a flicker of hope—or was it just madness?

I pressed my hands to my face, trying to stifle a sob. This wasn't who I was supposed to be. I was supposed to be strong, unwavering, driven by loyalty to my family and the memories of those we'd lost.

But Verno… he was starting to become a crack in that armour.

And I didn't know how to stop it.

Outside, I could hear the murmur of voices—Damion's deep timbre mingled with Verno's. I peered through a small gap in the tent, catching a glimpse of Verno's profile, his laughter soft but genuine as he spoke with the king.

I swallowed hard, my heart a traitorous flutter in my chest.

No, I thought to myself. *I can't let him get under my skin.*

Because if I did, it wouldn't just be my heart on the line.

It would be everything I'd fought to protect.

Thirty-Two

Melody

⁂

The camp buzzed with frantic energy. Men and women rushed about, loading boxes into caravans, saddling horses, and calling orders back and forth. The air was thick with tension, the kind that made my skin crawl.

'What's going on?' I demanded, stepping into the chaos.

Damion stood near the largest caravan, his arms crossed and his gaze sharp. He didn't look at me right away, as if I weren't worth his attention. 'It's time to go,' he said coolly. 'The soldiers have retreated.'

I froze. 'Soldiers were here? Looking for us?'

He finally turned to me, a smirk tugging at the corner of his mouth. 'And you didn't notice?'

'You didn't tell me!' I snapped, taking a step toward him. 'Was there anyone—'

'They weren't sent by your father.' His smirk vanished, replaced by a more serious expression. 'It was Aria's fiancé who sent them.'

The pit in my stomach twisted tighter. 'Oh.'

'Have you heard anything from home?' I asked quickly, hoping to deflect.

'Yes.'

I leaned closer, my heart pounding. 'And?'

'I'm not telling you, Melody.'

I glared at him, my jaw tightening. 'You're so lucky I promised Aria I wouldn't kill you.'

'And you're lucky I promised Verno to deliver you both unharmed to your aunt,' he shot back, a hint of amusement in his voice. 'So, we're even.'

'Hilarious,' I muttered.

'Aren't I?'

I hesitated, narrowing my eyes. 'What happens when I go back to my father?'

His gaze dropped to the ground for a moment, a flicker of something softer breaking through his usual indifference. 'I gave you the choice, Mel. I tried to save you from this war. But if you return to him… well, then it's war.'

'Friendships don't matter?' I whispered, my voice trembling.

'It's not personal, Mel.'

Anger boiled in my chest. I stepped closer, my fists clenched. 'No? You just want to take my father's life, my throne, my kingdom?'

His head shot up, his eyes blazing with fury. 'Your father killed the Demonic Court. He pushed them into my lands and seized their territories for himself! He did the same to the Angels. He won't stop!'

'You're lying!' My voice trembled, but it was edged with defiance. 'My father would never do that. I'd know—'

'You?' He cut me off with a bitter laugh. 'The princess locked away in her tower all her life? Sweetie, you don't even know what's happening in your own court, let alone your kingdom.'

Fury surged through me, and before I could think, my hand flew up. The sharp crack of my palm against his cheek echoed in the chaos around us. His head snapped to the side, but he didn't retaliate.

'I'm packing,' I hissed, turning on my heel.

* * *

The tension was still simmering beneath my skin as I sat by the fire, twisting the edges of my cloak between my fingers. The flickering light painted everything in shades of orange and gold, but it couldn't chase away the shadows clawing at my thoughts.

'I'm sorry, Aria, I am just worried,' I murmured, barely able to meet her gaze.

She leaned in, her expression soft with concern. 'Worried about what?'

'I feel like I'm betraying Kal,' I whispered, the words breaking something inside me as they left my lips.

Her arms were around me in an instant, holding me tight. 'No,' she said fiercely. 'Don't say that.'

'It's true.' My voice wavered as I clutched at her sleeve. 'He died before I could tell Father I loved him. I couldn't fight for him.'

'Mel...'

'I'm scared, Aria. Scared he's going to use you.'

Her brows furrowed. 'Use me? Who?'

'Damion,' I admitted, the name tasting bitter on my tongue.

'And Verno too. What if they're just using us? What if it's all a game?'

'Mel, stop.' Her voice was firm but kind. She cupped my face, forcing me to meet her steady gaze. 'You're trying to protect me. I love you for that, but this is my choice. I'm not afraid to take the risk. Okay?'

Her words hit me like a wave, leaving me breathless. Reluctantly, I nodded. 'Okay.'

'Good.' She smiled, brushing a tear from my cheek. 'Now stop worrying so much. You'll give yourself wrinkles.'

I laughed weakly, wiping my face. 'I hate you sometimes.'

'No, you don't.'

By morning, the camp was packed and ready to move. The sound of hoofbeats filled the air as Damion's men readied the horses. Damion approached, his expression grim.

'We need to move,' he said, his tone clipped. 'Your fiancé's men are close.'

'Reinforcements?' I asked, dread curling in my stomach.

'Yes. They're coming for Aria.'

'For Aria?' My voice rose with panic.

'Yes,' he snapped, his patience fraying. 'You're both pawns to your father's enemies and allies. You're leverage.'

The camp erupted into motion, the weight of his words pressing heavily on my chest. I watched him for a moment, my fists clenching at my sides, before I stepped forward.

'Damion,' I called, my voice sharper than I intended.

He turned, his gaze cold and guarded. 'Not now, Melody.'

'Now,' I insisted, stepping closer. 'I deserve to know the truth.'

He hesitated, then sighed. 'Your father destroyed my home. My family. My people. And now, I'm supposed to protect you because of a promise I made to Verno. Do you have any idea how much that kills me?'

I swallowed hard, my anger ebbing. 'Damion, I didn't know—'

'Of course, you didn't.' His voice was bitter. 'You were locked away, kept safe while the rest of us fought to survive like monsters.'

'You're not a monster,' I said quietly.

He stilled, his dark eyes searching mine. 'Could've fooled me.'

'I see you,' I said, surprising even myself. 'And I know you're trying.'

For a moment, the mask he wore slipped, and I saw something raw beneath it. He nodded, his voice soft. 'We need to move.'

As I followed him into the chaos, a flicker of hope sparked in my chest. Maybe we didn't have to be enemies. Maybe, just maybe, there was another way forward.

Thirty-Three

Aria

———✦———

'Where are we?' I asked, pressing my face against the carriage window to get a better view of the moonlit landscape.

'We're crossing into neutral territory,' Verno answered, his voice calm.

'To our aunt's?' I asked, a flicker of a smile lighting my face.

He nodded. 'Yes, but we'll rest here for the night.'

I glanced around, taking in the shadowy outlines of twisted trees and half-collapsed stone buildings. 'This place seems... very sketchy.'

'It is,' Verno replied. 'We're near the edge of the realm where the Demons live. They have no lands of their own, so they've made a home here in the borderlands—much like the Angels who live at the edge of the Light Fae's territory.'

I nodded slowly, remembering our childhood lessons. Our tutors had always glossed over the details of Angels and

Demons, dismissing them as remnants of diluted bloodlines with no crowns to wield or kingdoms to rule.

The moon was high, casting silver light over the crumbling ruins where we had set up camp for the night. The air was thick with the scent of damp earth and old moss, a chill breeze rustling through the shadows. Melody and I were tending to a small fire, trying to keep warm against the cold creeping in from the surrounding forest.

I glanced up, expecting to see Verno's dark figure keeping watch, but he was nowhere in sight. Damion had insisted he take a rest, though I knew Verno would rather stay vigilant.

That's when I heard it—a soft rustle, like the whisper of leaves, followed by an unsettling stillness.

'Mel, did you hear that?' I whispered, my voice barely more than a breath.

Before Melody could respond, a shadow erupted from the darkness, moving faster than I could react. A Demon, eyes glowing a sickly yellow, lunged straight toward me, claws outstretched.

'Aria!' Melody screamed, scrambling to her feet, but it all happened too quickly.

I threw my hands up, trying to summon my magic, but panic slowed my thoughts, the frost refusing to form. The demon's twisted grin was the last thing I saw before a blur of movement cut between us.

Verno.

He threw himself in front of me, his body colliding with the Demon's, sending both of them crashing to the ground.

'Get back!' he shouted, his voice rough and commanding. In one fluid motion, he pulled a dagger from his belt and drove it into the demon's shoulder. The creature howled in pain, its claws raking across Verno's arm, leaving deep, bloody gashes.

My heart lurched as I watched Verno struggle, blood dripping from his wounds. Without thinking, I reached out, ice surging from my fingertips to encase the demon's legs. The creature snarled, trying to break free, but the ice held firm.

'Aria, now!' Verno yelled, his voice strained.

I didn't hesitate. With a flick of my wrist, shards of ice shot out, piercing the demon's chest. It let out a final, guttural scream before collapsing, its body dissolving into a dark, acrid mist.

The silence that followed was deafening. I turned to Verno, who was slumped against a fallen pillar, clutching his bleeding arm.

'You… you saved me,' I stammered, my voice barely more than a whisper.

Verno's eyes met mine, dark and intense even as pain twisted his features. 'Of course I did,' he said, his voice rough. 'What kind of monster do you think I am?'

I rushed to his side, kneeling beside him. My hands hovered over his wounds, unsure if my magic could help. 'You're hurt.'

He winced but tried to wave me off. 'It's nothing.'

'Don't be stupid.' I tore a strip of fabric from my dress, pressing it against the worst of the cuts to stem the bleeding. 'Why did you… why did you do that?'

'Because,' he said softly, his voice low enough that only I could hear, 'there are more things at stake here than you realize.'

* * *

'Sit down. But you might not like what I have to say.'

Of course, she wouldn't let it go. Melody never did. She was relentless in her own way, cutting through walls I didn't even realize I was putting up.

'Fine,' I said, gesturing at the space across from me.

She didn't hesitate, folding herself onto the furs like it was a throne and not a half-frozen scrap of comfort.

Her confidence made me want to laugh and groan all at once. In the cramped warmth of the tent, with the sounds of the camp just beyond the thin walls, it felt like we were the only two people in the world. And for once, I couldn't decide if that was comforting or terrifying.

I watched Melody settle in, her sharp, expectant gaze fixed on me. The warmth of the lantern cast flickering shadows over her face, making her look softer, almost vulnerable, but I knew better. Melody could be steel-wrapped in silk when she wanted to be, and right now, she was waiting—no, demanding— answers.

I blew out a breath, running a hand through my hair. 'You don't let things go, do you?'

'Not when I know something's wrong,' she said, tilting her head. 'So? Out with it. You've been acting strange ever since the frost thing with Verno. I apologized; we talked about it, but you haven't gone back to being you yet.'

My stomach twisted at her bluntness. I hated how easily she saw through me, even when I was trying my best to keep things together. 'It's not about Verno,' I said, maybe too quickly.

Her eyebrows shot up. 'Oh? Because from where I was standing, it seemed like something was happening between you two.'

Heat rushed to my cheeks. 'It's not like that,' I snapped, even though I wasn't entirely sure if that was true. 'He's helping me with my magic. That's all.'

Melody leaned back slightly, her lips quirking into a small, knowing smile. 'Right. And the hug?'

I glared at her, though I could feel my blush deepening. 'It was… a moment. I was grateful, and he was just—' I stopped, my words catching in my throat. 'Why are you even asking me this?'

'Because I care,' she said, her voice softening. 'And because I've seen what happens when you bottle things up. You can't afford to keep doing that, Aria. Not with everything going on.'

'I still remember the day I accidentally froze Mother's garden,' I murmured, my voice heavy with guilt. 'Her roses turned to ice, brittle and broken, and the look on her face—like I'd destroyed something precious—it still haunts me.'

I stared at her for a moment, torn between brushing her off and letting the truth spill out. Melody could be infuriatingly persistent, but she wasn't wrong. She never was.

'I'm scared,' I admitted finally, the words slipping out before I could stop them. 'I'm scared of what my magic might do. I'm scared of what I might do. And Verno…' I shook my head, my hands knotting together in my lap. 'He makes me feel like I can handle it, but that's dangerous, isn't it? Letting someone get that close.'

Mel immediately knew the image that was conjured in my mind. 'Aria, you were a kid.'

'I'll never forget the way Kal's mother looked at me that day,' I said quietly, my voice trembling. 'I didn't mean to—her hand was on my shoulder, trying to comfort me after a tantrum, and then the frost spread. It crawled up her arm before I even realized what I'd done.' I swallowed hard, my fists clenching in my lap. 'She screamed, and when I pulled away, her skin was raw and red, like she'd been burned by ice. I tried to apologize, to fix it, but she just… looked at me. Like I was a monster.'

Melody didn't respond right away, her expression softening as she leaned forward. 'Aria,' she said gently, 'you're allowed to let people in. You're allowed to trust someone—even if it feels risky.'

'It's not that simple,' I said, my voice barely above a whisper. 'What if I hurt him? What if I hurt everyone?'

'You won't,' she said firmly, reaching out to place a hand over mine. 'I've seen what you're capable of, Aria. You don't give yourself enough credit. You're stronger than you think.'

I looked at her, blinking back the sting of tears. 'And if I'm not?'

'Then you've got me,' she said with a small smile. 'And Verno. And the rest of us. We're not going to let you fall apart.'

Her words wrapped around me like a lifeline, steady and sure, and for the first time in what felt like forever, I believed her. Melody had always been stubborn, but it wasn't just for herself—it was for the people she cared about, too. And right now, that included me.

'Thanks,' I said, my voice shaky but sincere.

'Always,' she said, squeezing my hand before letting go. 'Now, are you going to admit you have feelings for Verno, or do I have to drag it out of you?'

I groaned, throwing my hands up in exasperation. 'Melody!'

She laughed, a bright, genuine sound that filled the tent. 'What? I'm just saying, he looked at you like you hung the moon. It's cute.'

I couldn't help but smile, even as I rolled my eyes. 'You're impossible.'

'And you love me for it,' she said with a wink. 'Now, come on. Let's go find something to eat before Damion yells at us for being late again.'

She stood and pulled me to my feet, her energy infectious despite the weight of everything looming over us. For a moment, the world outside the tent didn't matter. There was just us, two sisters in arms, holding each other up when it felt like everything was about to fall apart.

And somehow, that was enough.

Thirty-Four

Melody

We rested in a hidden camp. Verno returned from a scouting mission with grim news. 'Your father's army is on the march,' he told us. 'They'll reach your Aunt's borders in less than a week.'

'And my aunt?' I asked, her voice trembling. 'Will we make it in time?'

Damion's jaw clenched. 'We'll try. But if your father's forces intercept us… we fight.'

My heart sank. 'There has to be another way.'

Damion's dark eyes met mine, a storm brewing within them. 'You still don't understand, do you? This isn't just about us. If your father wins, the kingdoms will burn.'

'Then let me help,' I said, surprising myself. 'Let me speak to him. Negotiate. If there's even a chance—'

'There's no negotiating with a tyrant,' Damion snapped, his voice rising. 'He won't listen to you, Mel. He'll use you.'

'I have to try,' I said, her voice steady despite the fear coursing through her. 'You've spent years fighting him, and it's only made things worse. Let me do something different.'

For a long moment, Damion stared at her, his expression unreadable. Then he turned away, his voice low. 'Do what you want. But don't expect me to save you if it fails.'

The tension hung thick in the air, stifling and unrelenting. Damion's words lingered like an echo, slicing through the fragile quiet of the camp. His back was to me now, his shoulders taut as he walked away, leaving me standing there, uncertain and trembling.

'Mel,' Aria said softly, her voice pulling me from my spiralling thoughts. She stepped closer, her hand brushing mine. 'Are you sure about this?'

'No,' I admitted, the word falling from my lips like a stone. 'But if I don't try, what's left? Another battlefield? Another round of senseless bloodshed?'

Her expression wavered, sympathy mixing with the same doubt I felt in my gut. She didn't press me, though. Aria had seen enough to know when words wouldn't help.

'We'll leave at first light,' Damion called over his shoulder, his voice sharp and final. 'Make sure you're ready.'

The camp broke in silence the next morning. The air was crisp, the first signs of autumn painting the forest in hues of gold and amber. Horses snorted and pawed the ground, their breath was visible in the cool air as Damion's soldiers packed up supplies with practised efficiency. I stayed close to Aria, my hands busy with nothing in particular—adjusting my saddle, tying and retying my cloak—anything to avoid the knot of nerves growing in my stomach.

Verno returned from the tree line, his boots crunching softly over frost-dusted leaves. His expression was grim but less urgent than the night before. 'The scouts report no sign of your father's forces yet,' he told Damion. 'They're still two days behind us, at best.'

'That gives us time,' Damion said, tightening the straps on his horse's bridle. His tone was measured, but I caught the flicker of relief in his eyes.

'Time to get to my aunt,' I said, daring to hope.

'Time to prepare,' Damion corrected, his gaze cutting to me. 'Don't mistake a delay for safety, Melody.'

I bit back a retort and focused on mounting my horse. His scepticism was nothing new, but it stung all the same. He thought I was naive, that my optimism was a weakness. Maybe he was right. But I had to believe there was another way—a way to end this without more lives lost.

The day passed in slow, steady travel. The forest was dense, the canopy above casting dappled shadows over the narrow trail. The sound of hooves crunching through leaves and the occasional murmur of conversation filled the air, but otherwise, the group was subdued. Every step closer to the Fae Kingdom brought new layers of tension, a feeling that something—anything—could go wrong at any moment.

* * *

I found myself riding next to Verno as the afternoon wore on. He was quiet, as usual, his sharp eyes scanning the trees for signs of danger. For a while, I said nothing, content to let the rhythm of travel fill the space between us. But eventually, the silence became too much.

'Do you think I'm wrong?' I asked, keeping my voice low. 'About trying to negotiate?'

Verno didn't answer right away. He guided his horse over a fallen log, his movements deliberate. 'I think you're brave,' he said finally. 'But bravery doesn't always mean you're right.'

'That's not very reassuring,' I muttered, earning a faint smile from him.

'It wasn't meant to be,' he said. 'But if anyone could surprise me, it's you.'

I looked at him, startled by the rare warmth in his tone. He wasn't mocking me or dismissing me like Damion so often did. He was… encouraging me, in his own quiet way.

'Thanks,' I said softly, feeling a small flicker of confidence in his words.

We reached the edge of the Fae Kingdom just as the sun began to sink below the horizon, painting the sky in deep shades of orange and violet. The forest thinned here, giving way to rolling hills shrouded in mist. A towering stone arch, weathered and overgrown with ivy, marked the border itself. Beyond it, the landscape seemed to hum with an unnatural stillness, as if the very air was holding its breath.

Damion called for a halt, dismounting and gesturing for the others to follow suit. 'We'll camp here tonight,' he said. 'Crossing into the Fae lands after dark isn't worth the risk.'

The soldiers murmured their agreement, and the group began setting up camp. I lingered near the arch, staring up at its intricate carvings—symbols I didn't recognize, but that felt ancient and powerful. The faintest shimmer of magic crackled along its edges, making the hair on my arms stand on end.

'Second thoughts?' Aria's voice startled me, and I turned to see her standing a few feet away, her expression curious.

'Not about this,' I said, gesturing toward the arch. 'But everything else? Constantly.'

She chuckled, the sound soft but genuine. 'That's normal. It means you care.'

'Caring feels like a liability right now,' I admitted.

'It's not,' she said, stepping closer. 'It's what makes you… you. And that's what we need, Mel. Someone who doesn't just see the fight but sees the people caught in it.'

Her words stayed with me long after she walked away. As the camp settled into a quiet rhythm, I found myself staring at the arch again, the mist swirling around its base like a silent invitation. The Fae Kingdom was just beyond it, the answers I sought closer than ever.

For the first time in weeks, hope didn't feel quite so out of reach.

Thirty-Five

Aria

The carriage jolted again, throwing me slightly off balance. I gripped the edge of the seat, glaring at Verno, who sat across from me, lounging like the uneven road was nothing more than a mild inconvenience. He smirked at me, that maddening, infuriating smirk that seemed to say he found my discomfort amusing.

'You know,' I said, my voice sharp, 'you could at least pretend this ride isn't comfortable.'

'It's not,' he replied with an indifferent shrug. 'But complaining won't make it smoother.'

'I'm not complaining,' I shot back.

'Of course not,' he said, his smirk deepening. 'You're just… offering commentary.'

I let out an exasperated sigh and leaned back against the cushions. Every bump and sway of the carriage reminded me of how far we still had to go, and the weight of the journey hung heavy over me. The Fae Kingdom was days away, but the distance wasn't what bothered me. It was the uncertainty. What kind of reception would we face? What would happen when we arrived? And would this fragile alliance between Melody, Damion, and my father's enemies hold, or would it collapse under the weight of old grudges and new fears?

Verno didn't seem to care about any of it. Or at least, he didn't show it.

He leaned casually against the side of the carriage, one arm draped over the window frame. He wasn't trying to seem intimidating or aloof. It was just how he was—steady, unshaken, and aggravatingly unreadable. But beneath the irritation, I had to admit something I didn't want to. His presence, even with all its infuriating quirks, was comforting.

That was the problem.

'Why do you do that?' I blurted out, unable to hold the question any longer.

He raised an eyebrow, clearly intrigued. 'Do what?'

'Watch me,' I said, my words coming out sharper than I'd intended. 'You're always watching me.'

He didn't flinch or look away. Instead, he leaned forward slightly, his dark eyes meeting mine. 'Maybe I find you interesting,' he said, his voice calm and maddeningly smooth. 'Or maybe I'm just making sure you don't run off and do something reckless.'

I glared at him. 'I don't need a babysitter.'

'Good thing I'm not one, then,' he replied with a grin.

'You're impossible,' I muttered, crossing my arms over my chest.

'And you're deflecting,' he said, his smirk fading into something more serious. His gaze softened slightly as he tilted his head. 'What's really bothering you?'

His question caught me off guard. I hesitated, unsure if I wanted to answer. The words were there, just waiting to spill out, but saying them felt too vulnerable. Too raw. I glanced out the window, watching the trees blur into streaks of green and brown.

'Do you ever think about… your past?' I asked, my voice quieter now. 'About mistakes you've made?'

'All the time,' he said without hesitation. 'You?'

I laughed bitterly, the sound hollow. 'Yeah. Especially lately.'

He didn't push me, and for that, I was grateful. But the silence between us felt too heavy, so I decided to just let it out.

'Besr,' I said, the name tumbling from my lips like a stone.

His posture stiffened slightly, but he kept his gaze steady. 'Yeah. Him.'

I didn't know why I was telling him this, but once I started, I couldn't stop. 'I thought he loved me,' I said, the words trembling as they escaped. 'At first, it felt like he did. He was charming, kind. He made me feel… seen. But then he changed.'

Verno leaned forward, his voice careful. 'How?'

The memories clawed their way to the surface, each one sharper than the last. 'He was possessive. Controlling. It started small—little things, like telling me what to wear or who to talk to. But then it became… suffocating. If I didn't listen, he'd—' I broke off, my throat tightening.

'Did he hurt you?' Verno's voice was calm, but there was an edge to it, a quiet fury that made my chest tighten.

I shook my head slowly. 'Not physically. But the things he said, the way he made me doubt myself… it hurt.'

Verno's hands curled into fists on his lap, his jaw tight. 'I would kill him if I could.'

His words startled me, and I blinked at him. 'It doesn't matter now. He's not here.'

'It matters,' he said firmly, his voice low and steady. 'You matter.'

The sincerity in his tone left me breathless. No one had ever said something like that to me before—not with such conviction. Not even Besr.

'I didn't realize it was toxic until it was too late,' I admitted. 'I thought it was my fault, that I wasn't good enough. But now...' I turned to Verno, my voice steadying. 'Now I see it for what it was. And I don't want that kind of love ever again.'

'You deserve better,' he said, his dark eyes locking onto mine. 'You deserve someone who sees you for who you are and doesn't try to change you. Someone who's your equal.'

His words hit me like a blow, but not in a bad way. They stirred something deep within me, something I wasn't ready to name. 'And what about you?' I asked softly. 'What do you deserve?'

A faint smile tugged at his lips, though it didn't reach his eyes. 'I don't know. Maybe nothing. But if I ever find someone like you...' He trailed off, shaking his head. 'Forget it.'

'No,' I said quickly, my heart pounding. 'Say it.'

He hesitated, then leaned closer, his gaze holding mine. 'If I ever find someone like you, Aria, I'd do everything in my power to be worthy of her.'

The carriage jolted again, but I barely noticed. My world had narrowed to him—his words, his eyes, his presence. For the first time in years, I felt like someone wasn't trying to control me or fix me. Verno saw me as I was, and for once, I didn't feel the need to apologize for it.

'Maybe you already have,' I said softly, the words slipping out before I could think.

His eyes widened slightly, surprise flickering across his face. Then he smiled—a real, genuine smile that made my chest ache in a way I didn't entirely hate.

The rest of the ride passed in a tentative peace. The weight of my past felt a little lighter, and for the first time in a long while, the road ahead didn't feel quite so daunting.

Thirty-Six

Melody

'Time to go, girls,' Damion called softly, his voice barely louder than a whisper, as if afraid to disturb the fragile peace.

He gazed too long at the dress I wore. It was similar to the outfit that was prepared for me the first time I attempted this journey and Jas painstakingly applied the Ink for the painted roses on my skin. But unlike the court-appropriate dresses from my court, Jas had given me a dress in the Fae style, one made of black and red tulle; there were no sleeves, allowing my Inkings and arms to be completely on show.

I huffed in irritation, embarrassed by the royal attire I donned, gathering my skirts in a dramatic sweep as I stepped out of the carriage. 'Damion, if you value your life, don't speak to me right now.'

Damion flinched, his eyes dropping to the ground, looking like a scolded child.

I inhaled deeply as I stepped out of the carriage, the familiar, sweet scent of roses and sugar filling my senses. No matter how many times I visited, the beauty of the Fae kingdom always took my breath away. The pink trees, the shimmering blue and purple grass stretching as far as the eye could see—it was a world painted in dreamlike hues.

As I stepped out, I noticed my aunt waiting for us by the grand, golden gates. I was always surprised by how much we did truly looked alike, although her and my mother weren't twins, they still shared the same features. Just like me and Aria, the only difference were her pure purple eyes and dark black hair. She kept her wings hidden underneath the red cloak that was tied to her. Her regal presence seemed to radiate light amidst the fantastical landscape.

'Your Majesty,' Aria greeted, kneeling respectfully.

But she quickly pulled her up into her arms. 'Oh, Aria, stop with these formalities.' She pulled me a moment later, her embrace warm and familiar, and for a moment, I allowed myself to feel safe.

'Come,' she said, taking my arm as we walked through the gates. The palace grounds were alive with creatures of all kinds—some resembling us, others with wings or entirely different forms, all beautiful in that ethereal, lethal way that only Fae could be. They were creatures you couldn't look at for too long without losing yourself.

As we walked through the grand halls, I whispered to my aunt, 'You have no quarrel with him?'

She shrugged, a graceful lift of her shoulders. 'It is not my war. And we are Fae, we stand together.'

'But he is my father,' I said bluntly, searching her eyes for any flicker of loyalty.

Her expression softened. 'And I've been trying to take you away from him since you were born. You may not see it now, but your father is not a kind man.'

'I know that,' I muttered under my breath, my resolve wavering.

My aunt's eyes glimmered with something unsaid. 'Damion has been a friend to me for years. You know Fae age differently. Truthfully, I had hoped for you two to marry, but… he was never legitimized. Ruby was made regent last year.'

I looked at her curiously. 'Why not?'

She smirked, a knowing look in her eyes. 'That is his story to tell. His father never married and never took a queen. Thus, his mother was never recognized as a lady of any standing.'

I nodded slowly. 'Yet he is still the King of the Dark Fae.'

'Yes,' she said with a smile. 'Dark Fae may have chaotic power, but it doesn't mean they possess dark hearts. Their court, in fact, is quite delightful.'

As we entered the grand ballroom, my aunt called out, 'Ali, come say hello to your cousins!'

Ali rushed forward, embracing me tightly. 'Mel!' She then turned to my sister. 'Aria!'

Ali was strikingly beautiful, with curly locks of blonde hair pushed away from her small face by a black headband. She wore a simple blue and white dress, roses of ink running across her body to symbolize our family.

Then came Ruby, the strikingly beautiful Regent of the Dark Fae, we knew of her slightly through Ali, we knew she was the old King's chosen proxy at court. But that was all, really.

She raced into Verno's arms, her laughter echoing through the hall.

'Brothers,' she yelled out.

I raised an eyebrow at Aria. 'Brothers?'

My aunt simply shrugged. 'Ruby grew up in the Rose Court. She's Verno's sister through their mother. Her father was an old friend who passed away.'

'How are Verno and Damion brothers, then?' I asked.

'By their father,' my aunt whispered back.

I nudged Aria playfully. 'We can't say anything, but honestly, how do we not have more siblings with how our father carries on?'

Aria laughed softly, though her eyes were wary. My aunt continued, 'The king loved both their mothers, years apart. It's far more honourable than anything your father has done.'

'Aunt!' Aria protested, but I couldn't help but laugh as I watched the Fae siblings reunite.

As the evening wore on, Blanche, the Queen of the Light Fae, approached us. She was angelic, her hair a pure white and her eyes, a dark, unnatural pink. The Inkings of branches told me she was of a nature Fae family. I watched the way she looked at Verno and Damion, her expression guarded yet intrigued.

'Brothers?' I repeated to her, seeking clarity.

Blanche nodded slowly. 'Yes. It's important to maintain peace between our courts. We don't wish for a civil war.'

'But why would there be one?' I asked.

She sighed, her voice lowering. 'Verno's and Ruby's mother was a noblewoman, respected in the Fae court. Damion's… was a Demon.'

'A Demon?' I echoed, surprised. Suddenly the need for revenge clicked.

'Yes, though she was somewhat respectable among the Demon-folk. But Demons no longer hold any thrones or titles. Still, the court would prefer Verno. He was the commander of the army before his father's death, the son of a great family. Yet both bastards. Loyalists are a cruel, and unloving way to die.'

I tilted my head. 'And yet his mother's affair with their father nearly ruined them.'

Blanche's gaze sharpened. 'Precisely. To the world, they are known as his chosen family, dear friends he's taken in after the death of their parents. But the truth… the truth is dangerous.'

* * *

As the evening wound down, Damion led me onto the dance floor. His touch was light, but his eyes held a seriousness that sent a shiver down my spine.

'Stay safe, Melody,' he murmured as we twirled slowly. 'Don't get involved in the affairs of kings.'

I smiled bitterly. 'Even if I am to be a queen?'

His eyes softened, though his words were harsh. 'The sins of your ancestors should not dictate your rule. Start fresh. Let your reign be free of bloodshed.'

I leaned in closer, lowering my voice. 'Will you give my throne back to me, then?'

His expression tightened. 'That… it is unheard of for a Fae king to relinquish a throne, especially to a witch.'

'My mother was Fae,' I countered. 'But I have witch blood. The witches will never follow you.'

Damion's gaze darkened. 'Your father stole lands that belonged to the Dark Fae, he destroyed the Demons. He is mad, Melody, driven by hatred. He destroyed entire families.'

'He's still my father,' I said, my voice breaking.

Damion's eyes softened with something akin to pity. 'I can

protect you. You don't have to fight this alone.'

I pulled away, fire burning in my chest. 'I don't need your protection. This is my crown, my family. I'm going back.'

'No,' Damion said, his voice rising.

'No?' I repeated incredulously.

'You're going to declare war over a mad king?'

I smiled coldly. 'No, I'm going to declare war because I'm a spoiled brat not getting what I want.'

Damion's jaw clenched. 'Very well. But if you leave this court, I will offer you no kindness in the game of kings and queens. I have honoured my duty and our deal.'

I leaned in, pressing a kiss to his cheek. 'I would have it no other way, sweetie. I play to win.'

'We shall see,' he muttered, eyes glinting with a mix of anger and admiration.

'Goodbye,' I said, turning on my heel. As I walked away, I heard Damion call out behind me.

'Verno!' Damion shouted, his voice carrying through the grand hall as I made my exit.

And I couldn't help but smile.

Because the game had only just begun.

Thirty-Seven

Aria

⁓❧⁓

The scent of roses and fresh rain still clung to the air. The walls of the grand hall seemed to echo with every angry word we hurled at each other. The golden chandeliers above us sparkled with an unfeeling beauty, their light casting a warm glow on everything except the icy chasm that was opening between us.

'Aria, let's go!' Melody's voice was strained, her fingers gripping my arm as if she could physically pull me back into the life I was desperately trying to escape.

I pulled away, shaking my head. 'I am staying.'

Her eyes widened, desperation and disbelief swimming within them. 'Staying? Where?'

I swallowed hard, my voice a mere whisper. 'Here. In the Rose Court.'

Her grip tightened, almost bruising. 'But Aria... what's waiting for me back home? A tower? An engagement to a man who will control my every move?'

My resolve wavered for a moment. I could see the fear in her eyes, the fear that I was choosing something that would break me. But I couldn't go back to the life we had left behind. 'There's nothing left for me there, Mel.'

'What about me?' she whispered, her voice breaking. 'Am I nothing to you?'

That broke me. My throat tightened, tears burning behind my eyes. 'Mel, it doesn't involve us. I don't understand why you're going back. For a throne? For power? You don't have to fight their wars. You could rule if you must; just... give them their lands back. I have spent my life worrying about prophecies and curses; what if, by separating neither comes true?'

Her eyes blazed with fury. 'And you're fine with the blood spilled by our father? With the cruelty he inflicted?'

'Of course not!' I shot back, but my shoulders sagged under the weight of everything I couldn't fix. 'But Mel, what good would it do for us to get caught in the crossfire? I'm tired... so tired of fighting for a place in a world that doesn't want us.'

'There's me, Aria!' she shouted, her voice raw, eyes glistening with unshed tears. 'I need you! I can't do this alone.'

I stepped closer, reaching for her hand, but she pulled back, her expression a mix of heartbreak and anger. 'And I love you, Mel, but this fight... it isn't mine. It isn't yours either. Just because you're ready to go to war doesn't mean I have to be a soldier too. Can't we find happiness here, together?'

Her bitter laugh cut through me. 'Happiness? Here? In the arms of a man you barely know?'

Her words stung, but I forced myself to stay calm. 'It's not like that, Mel!'

'Of course, it isn't,' she said, her voice dripping with sarcasm.

'You always run, observe and be a good little wife, Aria. You always find some excuse to follow your heart, even when it leads you away from everyone who needs you. You are the one who told me I was selfish for not wanting to go back, for wanting till it all ends. And now it's you?'

I blinked rapidly, trying to hold back the tears that threatened to spill. 'Please, Melody, don't let this be how we part. I don't want to be enemies. What if we never see each other again?'

Her resolve seemed to falter, the anger in her eyes dimming. She took a step forward and pressed a soft kiss to my cheek, her lips trembling against my skin. 'You're right,' she whispered, voice barely holding together. 'Stay safe, Aria.'

'You too.' My voice broke, tears finally spilling down my cheeks as I reached out to touch her hand, but she pulled away, her eyes still glistening with unshed tears.

As we stood there, staring at each other, the air between us seemed to vibrate with all the words we couldn't say. Finally, she turned on her heel, wiping her eyes as she walked away, her shoulders stiff with anger.

'I'm still angry,' she called over her shoulder, not turning back to face me.

I managed a weak smile. 'As am I.' But deep down, my heart was breaking. Because despite everything we had gone through, despite all the battles we had fought side by side, this was one fight we would have to face alone.

I turned to find Verno watching us, his expression unreadable. His gaze was like a cloak around my shoulders—heavy, suffocating, and yet strangely comforting.

'Are we really going to let them tear themselves apart?' I asked, my voice barely more than a whisper.

He didn't answer immediately. His jaw was set, eyes dark and stormy. 'In the game of kings and queens, love is a luxury few can afford.'

His words cut deeper than I cared to admit. I wanted to argue, to tell him that love was worth fighting for, that I had just lost the only family I had left to protect the remnants of my heart. But the cold reality of our world made that argument seem childish.

Instead, I turned away, my shoulders slumping in defeat. As Melody's figure disappeared down the corridor, I realized that everything had changed. The choices we made today would ripple through our futures, and there was no going back.

But when I looked at Verno, the way his eyes softened when they met mine, the way his hand almost, but not quite, reached for mine… I wondered if maybe, just maybe, there was still something worth fighting for.

If only I was brave enough to reach out and take it.

'Let's go,' Verno said softly, his voice pulling me back to the present. I nodded, blinking away the tears that refused to stop falling.

The game of kings and queens had begun, and whether I wanted it or not, I was already a player.

And this time, I would make my own rules.

About the Author

Mimi Rose is a passionate storyteller who weaves enchanting worlds where romance and magic collide. A lifelong dreamer and avid reader of all things fantastical, she began crafting her own tales as a teenager, filling notebooks with stories of love, adventure, and the extraordinary.

Drawing inspiration from folklore, mythology, and the complexities of human connection, Mimi creates characters that are as flawed as they are endearing, set against vividly imagined landscapes. Her stories often explore themes of resilience, self-discovery, and the power of love to transform even the most broken of hearts.

When she's not writing, Mimi can be found curled up with a cup of tea and a good book, exploring the great outdoors, or daydreaming about her next fictional adventure. She lives in England, where she's hard at work on her next romantic fantasy novel.

Connect with Mimi on social media and join her journey into magical realms.